EQUINOX

TIME PATROL

BOB MAYER

COOL GUS

EQUINOX

TIME PATROL
by
Bob Mayer

"History will be kind to me, for I intend to write it."
Winston Churchill

THE TIME PATROL

There once was a place on our planet called Atlantis. Ten thousand years ago it was attacked by a force known only as the Shadow, on the same date, over the course of six years. The seventh attack obliterated Atlantis to the point where it is just a legend, but our ancestors managed to survive.

The Time Patrol now knows there are many Earth timelines, which all originated from a single timeline initiated by Atlantis because of some event prior to that destruction which the Time Patrol still doesn't know. The Shadow comes from one of those timelines where Atlantis still exists. It is attacking our timeline by punching bubbles into our past that last no more than twenty-four hours. In each bubble, the Shadow is trying to change our history and cause a time ripple.

By itself, a single time ripple can be dealt with and absorbed in the overall stream of history. A significant time ripple that is unchecked can become a Cascade. That changes history, but the timeline still survives.

However, six Cascades can combine to become a seventh, cataclysmic event: a Time Tsunami.

That would be the end of our timeline and our existence.

To achieve its goal, the Shadow attacks six points in time simultaneously, on the same date in different years.

The Time Patrol sends an agent back to each bubble in those six years to keep history the same. Despite losses, so far, they have succeeded.

This is one of those dates: **22 September.**

The Autumn Equinox falls between 21 and 24 September; but most often on 22 September. The Equinox is when the Sun is exactly above the Equator and day and night are of equal length.

THIS PARTICULAR DAY: 22 SEPTEMBER

NEW YORK CITY, 22 September 1776

Nathan Hale must have smelled the food because he paused and looked up. There were dark circles under his eyes from a sleepless night. "Yes?"

"Food, sir. And drink."

Hale shook his head. "I desire neither." His voice was barely above a whisper and the look in his eyes was one of dazed shock, which was understandable. "I requested a Bible last night but one has not been provided. But they send me spirits? To dull my wits, I suppose."

"A little can't hurt," Scout said, although she had no idea if it would do any good for the condemned man to get a buzz on.

She put the plate and decanter down next to the inkwell on the ground. She glanced over her shoulder but the guard had closed the door behind her. She knelt in front of him. He looked up, their eyes meeting.

"Has anyone contacted you?" Scout asked.

Hale was confused. "Who? About what?"

"Escape," Scout said.

"Are you with us?" Hale asked.

"I am a friend."

"Were you sent?"

"In a manner of speaking," Scout said.

Hale shook his head. "No. You aren't a friend. You're another of Major Rogers' tricks. He pretended he was with the cause in the tavern yesterday. He took me into his confidence. Then betrayed me. That man has no honor. He's a drunken lout."

A man spoke from behind. "Careful with the insults now."

Scout jumped to her feet and spun about, hand going for the dagger hidden in a sheath inside her petticoat. She didn't draw it though because Major Robert Rogers was standing there with a pistol in his hand.

"I didn't think you were just a serving girl," Rogers said, "and your words to the prisoner prove I am right. I think we should enjoy seeing two hanged today."

SALEM, MASSACHUSETTS. 22 September 1692

Lara reached the dark village square. A crude gallows dominated the area. A beam supported by wooden tripods on either end. The same as the one she'd seen on her last visit. Except for the eight nooses drooping from the beam.

Lara stood still, scanning the village. It was quiet, windows shuttered. The download gave her a best guess where the condemned were, but that wasn't her mission. History had written that eight would be hung at dawn and there was nothing she could do about that. Which, of course, wasn't true. There was a lot she could do if she wanted to violate the first rule of the Time Patrol and change history.

Where was Unity? The download was no help in that.

Lara closed her eyes and focused her mind.

She heard Pandora, standing nearby, say something, but the

'goddess' was background noise, of no significance at the moment. Lara was 'looking' for Unity Hale, recalling the young girl's aura during the last mission. There was no sense of her in the village, but Pandora's presence was distracting. Lara opened her eyes.

"Why are you here?" Lara demanded of Pandora. "You were around last time, but bugged out as soon as things got a little difficult. From what Scout told me, I figured you'd be tougher."

"You handled it," Pandora said. "After all, you're back."

"You knew I'd be here," Lara said. *Where was Unity?*

"She's not in town," Pandora said.

"I know that," Lara replied. "I wasn't asking you because my lips didn't move."

"But you were asking loudly in your head," Pandora said. "Might want to get some control over that."

"Screw you." Lara faced her. "You knew I'd be back. There was never any question when this came up as a mission that it would be mine. You're here for me."

"No," Pandora said. She pointed with her Naga staff to Lara's left rear. "I'm here for him."

Standing in the moonlight dappled shadows at the edge of Salem was Lukas. A Lukas.

"Hello, sister," he said.

WASHINGTON D.C.. 22 September 1862

"Because Sally Hemings told my predecessor that." The Keep retrieved the Book of Truths. She put it on the only clear part of a crowded desktop. Opened the cover, then carefully turned heavy pages made of parchment until she found the notation which was noted by a thin red ribbon book mark. "The entry was made in late 1826." She read the flowing script:

"On the 22nd Day of September, the Equinox in the year of Our Lord, Eighteen Hundred and Sixty-Two, there will be a visitor. Much as

President Jefferson had been foretold on the 4th of 1776, that there would be a visitor on the fiftieth anniversary of the Signing in 1826. This information was provided by Sally Hemings, an associate of President Jefferson during a brief visit to the Capitol."

"'Associate'?" Eagle repeated. "She was his slave and lover."

A tinge of red crept onto the Keep's face and she didn't meet Eagle's eye. "She had information." She continued reading. "*She spoke not only of the visitor who had been foretold, but a vision she had shortly afterward by what she claimed was an angel. Normally, such a statement would be considered frivolous but the specificity of the vision and the date and what was imparted is significant enough for me to note. Especially as it is consistent with what President Jefferson confirmed with his early entries about what happened on the 4th of July 1776 in the early morning hours in Philadelphia.*"

"That's it?" Eagle asked. "Just that someone is going to show up today?" An angel, which meant that a Valkyrie had paid Heming a visit.

"It *is* very strange that you've arrived today," the Keep noted. "It seems a confluence of events are merging."

"How so?" Eagle asked.

"Hemings not only predicted your arrival, she also brought something with her that she requested be kept secret until this particular day and the arrival of a visitor." The Keep opened a drawer and removed a leather bag. She pulled out a Jefferson Cipher.

"That was thrown into the fire at Monticello," Eagle said, even though he realized the inanity of the statement as the words came forth.

"One was according to the report," the Keep said. "But this was a twin, which Jefferson had hidden. Hemings knew where it was. She claimed he'd forgotten about it in his old age."

"Did this vision instruct Hemings to bring the cipher here?"

"Not just the cipher," the Keep responded. She opened

another draw and withdraw a wooden tube. "She used it to uncover the original, signed, Declaration of Emancipation. It rests inside."

MANCHESTER, NEW YORK. 22 September 1823

A Gate opened behind Lachesis. "Come along, Roland."

With three gold plates, Roland dutifully followed. They went through the Gate and into a time tunnel. They stepped out onto a verdant hillside covered with towering trees under a clear night sky.

"Same place, same time?" Roland asked. "Different timeline?"

"Yes," Lachesis replied.

"What are we doing?"

"You wouldn't understand," Lachesis said as she peered about.

"Is this my mission?" Roland said. "Are they still frozen back in my timeline?"

"You ask many questions," Lachesis said.

"You don't explain much."

"Why should I?"

"You've asked me for help," Roland said. "It would be polite."

Lachesis laughed. "The fate of worlds is at stake and you're concerned about politeness."

Roland went on alert. "We're being watched."

"Of course, we are," Lachesis said. She called out in a different language Roland didn't understand.

An old man dressed in a well-worn leather shirt embroidered with brightly colored shells walked out from beneath the trees, one hand held up, palm showing. His skin was bronze, his dark hair long and straight and streaked with grey. He replied to her in the same language.

He spoke with Lachesis for a few moments, at one point indicating Roland. Whatever the Fate said satisfied him because he turned and shouted an order. Four younger men carried a stone sarcophagus into the clearing and removed the lid.

Lachesis repeated her procedure, running her hands over the plates. She tapped one. "Roland. Replace this one with the middle one you're carrying."

He did as instructed. "Who are these people?"

"What your timeline calls Native Americans," Lachesis said. "Except in this timeline, settlers from other lands have not arrived in the Americas. Yet." She chuckled. "Naturally, the two continents aren't called the Americas either, but it's a long story, as the history of a timeline always is."

"Are you from a timeline?" Roland asked Lachesis as he finished swapping out the plate.

Lachesis peered at him in the moonlight. "Yes."

"So, you're human?"

"In a manner of speaking." She dismissed any further questions with a brusque wave of her hand. "We have several more timelines to visit and our time is short. Come."

"I got a mission," Roland said.

"You're doing it," Lachesis said. "This touches on your teammate's missions. Some of them at least."

"How?"

"You wouldn't understand."

Roland growled, but followed her. They went through the tunnel of time and stepped out of a gate into a disaster. The trees were blasted and torn; the earth scorched. Fires raged all about. Lachesis held up her rod and she and Roland were in a safe bubble amidst the ruin.

"Too late," Lachesis murmured. "Too late."

"I thought time was frozen?" Roland said.

"Only your timeline," Lachesis said.

Roland looked up, but the night sky was blocked by thick smoke. "The entire planet like this?"

Lachesis didn't respond. She opened another gate. "Come. Hurry. The Shadow has caught on."

AREA 51. 22 September 1947

At that moment, though, a Firefly went into one of the flamethrowers, taking control. The barrel turned toward the man who had it strapped on his back, despite his desperate efforts to stop it. It flared and the man screamed briefly before Moms fired, killing him. She emptied the magazine into the flamethrower and it exploded, sending shrapnel flying. The Firefly floated up and dissipated.

Moms felt a tug of pain on her side, but grabbed a full magazine off the body of a soldier, slamming it home. Colonel Thorn was next to her, both firing controlled bursts.

There was so much going on that Moms almost missed the most critical element. Fat Man was slowly rolling toward the Rift under the arch. Moms paused in shooting to understand what she was seeing, then realized a Firefly had gotten into the metal cradle the bomb rested on. The wheels were slowly trundling the ten thousand, three-hundred-pound bomb across the floor, animated by the presence of a Firefly.

"Colonel," Moms shouted, getting Thorn's attention. She gestured.

Together they fired at one of the metal wheels of the cradle. Their rounds ricocheted off, careening across the cavern. The noise in the cavern was deafening as Thorn's soldiers were shooting at different targets, but the objects that were possessed by Fireflies were pulling back, coalescing around Fat Man. Four heavy power cords controlled by Fireflies were wrapped around the bomb, helping to pull it toward the Rift.

Moms looked; the Demon Core was gone, already sucked in.

"Damn it!" Thorn exclaimed. He pulled the key out of his pocket.

"What are you doing?" Moms demanded, but Thorn ignored her.

He stuck the key in the covering, unlocked and flipped it up. He didn't hesitate, slamming his fist on the red button.

Nothing happened.

Moms was frozen for a moment, but as Thorn ran for Fat Man, she followed. They both leapt on top of the bomb as it passed into the Rift.

BERLIN. 22 September 1948

"What are you doing, kraut?" An American NCO with a military police armband strode toward Neeley. He had a nightstick in hand and did not look happy to see her up here. "If you're on a work crew, get your ass downstairs."

"*Excuse me*?" Neeley replied in German.

"Don't speak that kraut crap to me," the sergeant said. He stopped three feet away and appraised her.

Neeley held up the letter. "I have authorization from General—"

The sergeant cut her off. "So you do speak English." He laughed. "Right. Like the general would be giving you a letter." His eyes narrowed in thought and he looked about, making sure no one else was on the roof. With his free hand he reached into his pocket and pulled out a candy bar. "How 'bout you and me make a trade? I'll give you this and won't report you for being in a restricted zone and you give me—"

He didn't finish as Neeley attacked, her fist aiming for his throat. She was surprised as he dodged the blow and jabbed her in the solar plexus with the nightstick, knocking the wind out.

Neeley dropped to her knees, gasping for breath. The MP's

boot hit her in the chin with a snap kick, tumbling her onto her back. As she lay there, still trying to breath, stunned from the kick, he placed the boot on her chest, pressing down where the baton had already hurt her.

"I was told you would be a worthy opponent." He drew a knife, the sharp steel glittering. "I am sad that is not true. I am Legion and you will die slowly and with much blood."

BUT BEFORE EQUINOX, AND AFTER THEY CAME BACK FROM HALLOWS EVE

THE SPACE BETWEEN

The air was unpleasant; oily and thick and with an unnatural stillness as if there was never a wind or even a breeze.

Which there wasn't in the Space Between.

"Strange how you get used to it," Amelia Earhart said to Sin Fen.

The aviatrix appeared almost exactly as she had in her last photos before setting off on her round-the-world journey: short brown hair, wearing a one-piece flight suit that was well worn and patched; her face and hair slightly aged. A half-dozen Samurai wearing their armor of steel, leather and wood, armed with Naga staffs and swords, formed a loose perimeter around the two women.

"I try not to notice," Sin Fen said.

There was no sunlight in the Space Between. Illumination seeped through a gray haze above their heads, the origin unknown, but not solar or from a single source. It never went out, leaving the Space in a perpetual half-light. They were on the shore of a body of water, the Inner Sea, which extended as far as one could see, disappearing into the same haze, which indicated something suspended in the air; it definitely contributed to the odor and texture. The surface of the water was black and completely smooth, unmarred by waves or ripples. The water appeared as foul as the air smelled. Earhart had dubbed it the Inner Sea because this place was contained inside something much larger given the surrounding walls that rose up into the haze. What and where, she, and the others from various parallel worlds and times trapped here, had no idea.

Within sight were several shimmering black columns of varying diameters extending upward out of the water and into the overhead haze. These were portals between timelines, some active, some not. It was impossible to tell from the outside and an unsuited human trying to enter one not via a Gate would be incinerated.

The Space Between was exactly that: a crossroads of parallel Earth timelines. Amelia Earhart had been sucked into it during her infamous flight, but even she wasn't certain which Earth timeline she was from. Occasionally she ran into someone who told her that in their timeline, she'd succeeded. She hadn't pursued that further because she didn't want to know about a life that would never be hers.

She was trapped here along with the samurai from centuries before her time. There were others in this netherworld from various eras and timelines. Most avoided contact, eking out a bare existence from crops in shallow valleys in the dark sandy soil between the Inner Sea and the wall. Fresh water came from small streams flowing out of the wall and into the Sea. The wall arced up and inward, indicating a huge enclosed space. What was on the other side of that wall was unknown.

Earhart had tried circumnavigating the Inner Sea on foot, but she kept getting recursed back to this same stretch of black sand even though she'd kept the Sea to the same side.

It was a timeless existence and Earhart had no idea how long she'd been here, but she had not aged in concurrence with the current time on Earth since her disappearance. The samurai were from Feudal Japan and had been on a sailing ship that had gone into a portal in the Devil's Sea, a patch of the Pacific Ocean southeast of Japan.

Sin Fen's origins were vaguer, along with her intermittent role as she spent time in the Space Between and elsewhere. Whether she went beyond, into other timelines, was a matter of speculation among Time Patrol team members. She was six feet, slender, and wore tight black slacks and a flowing red blouse, along with heavy boots. A Naga dagger was tucked into a wide leather black belt. She was a mixture of races: Chinese, Cambodian, Thai, French and others that had produced high cheekbones and almond-shaped eyes. Her skin was smooth and dark, making it difficult to determine her age.

"What is so urgent?" Sin Fen asked. "I came as quickly as I could once Dane received your message."

Not far away was a rusting freighter, the *Cyclops*, which had disappeared in the Bermuda Triangle in 1918. Next to it were five TBM Avengers in mint condition: the infamous Flight 19. Scattered along the shore or half sunk in the lake were ships and craft ranging from ancient times to a modern yacht. Other aircraft, even a dirigible, was beached in the distance.

"There's been a significant increase in Valkyrie movement," Earhart said.

"Another attack on my timeline?" Sin Fen asked.

"Likely," Earhart said. "If so, your analysts will pick up the historical ripples soon enough for your team to mount a mission into the bubbles when they open."

"What else?"

One of the samurai called out an obvious warning in his native tongue.

Earhart grabbed Sin Fen's elbow and led her to the *Cyclops*. There was a crack in the hull and the two women and the warriors slipped inside.

"There." Earhart pointed as a squad of figures in white armor floated by, two feet above the black sand. "Watch."

When Valkyries went to Earth via Gates, people often mistook them for angels. But it was the armor that allowed them to enter the gates in the Space Between unscathed. The helmets had no facial features other than red orbs for optics. A mane of red hair was attached to the back of the helmet: a trophy of hairs of victims woven together and dyed.

They had sharp, bladed claws on the end of their hands and some carried Naga staffs: a spear with a pointed, broad tip on one end and a small seven headed snake pommel on the other. They were humans from the Shadow's world, but the few who had been captured proved to be disfigured and in poor shape, with skin grafts and organ replacements. It seemed even with the armored suits, traveling through the portals took a toll on the body. How the suit hovered had not yet been figured out by the Acme support personnel at Area 51. Some suits had been hijacked by outcasts from the Russian Time Patrol, the Ratnik, who'd been affected by the Chernobyl disaster many years previously and set up their own base in the Space Between where they'd scavenged bodies from timelines to keep themselves alive.

These Valkyries, however, were from the Shadow, since the Time Patrol, with Earhart and her warriors' help, had wiped out the rogue Ratnik on their very first mission. Why the Valkyreies had to come through the Space Between rather directly through Gates between timelines not requiring protective suits, was another mystery the Time Patrol had yet to understand.

In the center of the squad, two Valkyries had a stone box

suspended from poles between them. The Valkyries shifted direction, heading over the black water toward a black column and disappeared into it.

"That's the fifth time we've seen something similar over—" Earhart paused, unable to quantify time in a place where there were no days or nights—"a relatively short period. I've been calling in our kin, our fellow seers, in all the timelines I have communication with, to warn them."

"What's in the box?" Sin Fen asked.

"A refugee party came through after one of those Valkyrie flights in a cannibalized suit. Warned us. The box contains gold plates. On the plates are etched various messages, some of which make no sense, but at the core, if one can decipher the hieroglyphics and also understand the physics, are the scientific basics for creating a Rift. The Valkyries are leaving the boxes in timelines' pasts to be found."

Sin Fen frowned. "Why would the Shadow be doing that?"

"Chaos," Earhart said. "The plates contain incoherent messages about the universe; but with enough material that someone could make something of it. A new cult, a new belief system, a new religion brought by angels. But the science that is mixed in? For a civilization at the right level of technology, a scientist could understand the keys to opening a Rift. Remember what happened in your timeline when Rifts opened?

"We encountered Fireflies," Sin Fen said, "which would take over inanimate objects. But beyond being a local threat they weren't a global threat. Then the Nightstalkers were formed. They would shut them."

"Yes, because you caught on early enough and responded appropriately," Earhart said. "Other timelines have been destroyed by what came through the Rifts. There's worse on the other side of the Rifts. The Shadow's timeline isn't the only evil one. There are others. Places where life on Earth developed differently. The

Shadow is causing chaos by instigating the opening of Rifts and having timelines attack each other. An effective strategy."

"Have they sent the box to our timeline yet?"

"It happens in concurrence with a simultaneous attack on a day," Earhart said. "The next mission your team gets, one of them will most likely be about the plates. But there could be something else. This activity is unprecedented since I've been here."

Sin Fen nodded. "Besides your warning, I've sensed an attack is coming to my timeline. Thank you. I'll let Dane know to be prepared."

CENTRAL PARK. NEW YORK CITY

"The tall, leggy lass already shown me this," Angus told Moms, as they stood in front of Cleopatra's Needle.

The artifact is located behind the Metropolitan Museum of Art in Central Park and often overlooked by tourists, despite being sixty-nine feet tall and weighing over two-hundred tons. Carved from red granite, its sides are scrolled with faded hieroglyphics.

The elderly Scotsman and middle-aged American woman made for an odd couple, yet curiously similar in aura. Angus was six feet tall, Moms a shade shorter. He was solidly built, with a barrel chest. He sported a gray beard and his exposed skin was leathery. Moms was broad-shouldered and narrow hipped. She had short brown hair which was grayer than before the previous mission she'd gone on. One or two more and the gray would outnumber the original color.

"Edith Frobish," Moms gave a name to the lass he'd mentioned. "She's our art historian and researcher."

"Legs and brains," Angus said. "Dangerous combination."

"I know you were in the Super-Max for some years, Angus," Moms said, "but times have changed. Women aren't spoken of in that manner anymore."

"You mean it's not politically correct to speak so," Angus said. "I've never been one to be such. Besides, it was a compliment and ought be considered as such. Nothing of ill intent meant. And that lecture is not why you have me here. Nor why you've had me at Fort Bragg the last few months being updated on all the latest widgets and gadgets in the arsenal. Impressive stuff those twisted souls have come up with, but it's still the mind that's the most formidable weapon."

Moms indicated the obelisk. "If you ask Edith, she'll tell you the story of the Needle, who made it and why and how it was shipped across the Mediterranean and the Atlantic, then hauled across Manhattan and put into place."

"A boring story it sounds," Angus said. "I'm sure she has better."

"Depends," Moms said. "I found it interesting that Cleopatra had nothing to do with the Needle but it bears her name. It was erected well before Cleopatra's time in 1475 B.C.. The stone was carved out of a quarry close to the first cataract of the Nile. Floated down river. Another, later pharaoh, did many of the hieroglyphics to celebrate victories but still before her time."

"I'd prefer a story with Cleopatra in it," Angus said. "She must have been a very special lass to sway kings and emperors and generals to her will. Or is such talk also frowned upon in modern society?"

"She was quite interesting to meet, especially on the Ides," Moms said. "Most don't know she was outside Rome on that day, in one of Caesar's villas."

Angus pretended to keep studying the hieroglyphics as if he understood them for several moments as he processed what she'd just said. "Why do they call you Moms?"

"We're all given a new name, a new identity when we join the team," she said. "Whoever we were before, is gone. The team choses the name."

"Because you take care of them," Angus said. "Is there a Fathers? Perhaps Pops as you Americans would say?"

Moms gaze grew distant in remembrance. "We had a man who'd been named Nada. He fit the bill."

"Word choice. 'Had'. Sorry to hear that. He must have been a special man to lead you lot." He turned toward her. "You're telling me you've met Cleopatra? Face to face?"

"Yes."

"Intriguing. Anyone else I might have heard of?"

"I was present when Thomas Jefferson died at Monticello in 1826."

"I saw the Rolling Stones in concert a long time ago," Angus said. He walked over to a bench facing the needle and sat.

Moms joined him, waiting for his explanation.

Angus stretched his legs out. "The last song they played was *Sympathy for the Devil*. Know it?"

"I've heard it."

"Are you like the devil? Present at deadly events? Ides of March? The expiration of Thomas Jefferson?"

"I never thought of it that way. We tend to go to key moments in history on our missions. Rarely are they happy events."

"Your man Orlando was a solid operator long ago before the memories took him to drink," Angus said. "Your Eagle fellow seems steady and grounded. I've enjoyed the company of your Edith; a very smart woman with deep knowledge. Ivar might know computers and such, but as an operator he leaves quite a lot to be desired. But none of you seem the type to wear tin foil hats."

"Should I be wearing one?" Moms asked.

Angus pointed at the Needle. "This is important, correct?"

"Correct."

"And Edith is an art historian, correct?"

"Correct."

"She checks it? The Needle?" He pointed to the right at the bulk of the Museum of Modern Art. "And the art inside."

Moms nodded. "Orlando chose well."

"That woman, oddest of the lot of you, Sin Fen, told me you were the Time Patrol, but I wasn't quite sure if she was a bit daft. She's certainly not an ordinary woman in any sense of the word. That Possibility Palace I was at briefly before being shipped off for training could have been an elaborate hoax, but it wasn't."

"It wasn't," Moms said. "And you and I are heading back there now. There's more you need to know."

"Such as?"

Moms glanced around. "We go back in time. Always back. Never forward. The future is unknown. But the past is fluid."

"Meaning it can be changed."

"Yes. Our mission is to keep history as recorded."

Angus pondered that for a moment. "Meaning someone's trying to muck with it. I ran into that with Ivar, yes?"

"Yes. When that happens, it's six attacks on the same day, in different years." Moms watched Angus to make sure he was understanding. "Each mission is for that day only. We send one agent to each bubble in time where the Shadow is trying to change history."

"Your job is to keep things as we think they were," Angus said. "But are we sure we know our history that well?"

"Fair point," Moms allowed. "We do the best we can to stop the change. We have analysts, specialists in every era of human history. Some of them even come from that era. You'll see the Pit shortly in the Possibility Palace. All of recorded history is kept track of."

Angus asked the obvious, that every recruit did, sooner or later. "Why not change things for the better?"

"Because we're still around," Moms said. "Lots of timelines aren't. We know ours has worked with the history it has. You'd be surprised how easy it is for mankind to destroy itself. Doing what appears to be the right thing at the time could be catastrophic."

Angus laughed. "Oh, my dear, I would not. I've seen the darker side of human nature many times. Even worse, is the stupid side. You're saying you prefer the known mistakes over the unknown disasters."

"Yes."

"It's always the same? Six missions? Same day? Different years?"

"Pretty much," Moms said. "There have been a few wrinkles now and then."

"Like what I did with Ivar. Occurring in the present?"

"Yes. That was unusual. There's a briefing book you can read in the team room on all the missions so far. Sometimes there are connections between missions that aren't obvious."

"Looking foward to it. I be thinking I'm here because you've taken casualties recently." It was not stated as a question.

"We have."

"My future was mightily locked in, pun intended," Angus said. "I've got nothing to lose."

"Your life."

"I've got nothing to lose." Angus stood. "Your Sin Fen lass didn't pick the right moment for my Choice."

"She's always right."

"No one is always right," Angus countered. "She said I could change the decision to kill my son's murderer. That was no choice at all. I've no regrets on the act. The real Choice would have been to prevent the murder."

"You didn't control that event."

"I could've warned my son."

"No, you couldn't have," Moms said.

Angus' face was as hard as the obelisk. "I'll take your word on it, then. When is it? Your Possibility Palace? The present?"

"I don't know," Moms admitted. "The location and time of the Possibility Palace is the most closely held secret in the Patrol."

"So secret you don't know." Angus nodded. "That's good security. Everyone talks under enough pressure, but one can't give up what they don't know."

Moms pointed at the obelisk. "Does it look solid to you?"

"It's stone. Plenty solid."

"It's slightly faded to me," Moms said.

Angus frowned. "The writing?"

"The stone." She turned toward the Metropolitan Museum. "I called you here because those of us who've traveled in time can see things others can't. Time travel affects us in some way. The slight fading of the Needle in my vision means a mission is imminent. You need to get up to speed before the alert arrives, but it's imminent."

"Let's be moving then."

AN ISLAND OFF THE COAST OF PUERTO RICO

"You know what they say," Neeley said. "You've got to get right back on the horse."

"I didn't fall off a horse," Roland responded, furrowing the barbed wire tattoo on his forehead as he glared at the surf lapping the beach. "I drowned." The tattoo covered an old scar from a pre-Time Patrol, pre-Nightstalker mission when Roland was in the army. That seemed forever ago.

"It was a metaphor," Neeley said. "That means--"

Roland cut her explanation off. "Eagle explained metaphors to me long ago, back at the Ranch. I didn't like the water before I drowned, I like it even less now."

"Then why did you come here with me?" Neeley asked.

They were on a small island off the coast of Puerto Rico. Once upon a time, it had been an impact zone for naval bombardment practice. Large, ominous signs on buoys warned off the curious with dire threats. Security forces in swift boats were afloat around the island to enforce the warnings. This enclave had been thoroughly swept by EOD personnel years ago and then secured. There were many unexploded shells and bombs in the surrounding terrain, a very effective barrier to infiltration from land if someone came ashore elsewhere.

"Because you said you wanted to come here," Roland said.

Neeley rolled her eyes. "You could have said no."

"But I wanted to be with you," Roland said.

"You could have picked a place," Neeley said.

Roland's frown grew deeper, as if he had never considered such a possibility, which was true. "Really?"

Neeley indicated the beach and the small resort of scattered bungalows hidden in the treeline. "It's nice, but the biggest reason I like coming here is that its secure. Not many places are and we both need to relax. But I'm sure we can find a different place to go."

"With no water?"

"Just to drink," Neeley promised.

Roland relaxed; as much as he could. He was six foot six and all muscle. He wore cut off camouflage pants and no shirt. His skin was pale since he was rarely out in the sun like this. Numerous scars crisscrossed the exposed flesh on his torso. Neeley wore a one-piece suit, covering most of the almost completely healed scars from her last mission where she'd been tortured just before the Indian Prime Minister, Indira Gandhi was assassinated on 30 October, 1984. She was tall and lean with black hair trimmed short. Deep lines were etched at the side of her eyes, indicating a long and stressful life.

They lay next to each other, content for the moment, an unusual calm interlude for two efficient killers. The sounds of the surf was soothing, but it didn't seem to penetrate far into Roland.

"Do you think . . ." he began but lapsed into silence.

Neeley gave it a few moments. "Think what?"

"When I was drowning," Roland said, "I thought I'd be going to hell. If there is one."

"Why?"

"We've done terrible things," Roland said. "Killed people. Allowed bad things to happen."

"I never thought there was a hell," Neeley said. "Definitely not a heaven. Just cold dirt." Despite the bright sun, she shivered, remembering burying her former lover Gant on a hillside in Vermont many years ago. In the grave he'd dug for himself.

Roland instinctively reached around and put an arm around her, pulling her close.

"You're so smart," he said.

"That's because I'm older and wiser," Neeley joked.

"How old *are* you?"

"Oh, Rollie. You're never supposed to ask a woman that."

"Sorry. I was just a bit bummed thinking I might go to hell."

"Having traveled in time," Neeley said, "I'm not sure of anything. But if there is a heaven and hell, I don't think you'll be going to hell, Rollie."

"Why not?"

"You have a good heart."

"I've done bad things."

"For a good reason."

"I suppose. It confuses me sometimes."

"You're not the only one."

AFRICAN BURIAL GROUND NATIONAL MONUMENT. NEW YORK CITY

"I never knew this was here," Eagle said.

"Most New Yorkers don't," Edith Frobish, who'd adopted the city as her home years ago, said.

Eagle was a tall black man, his head devoid of hair, and the skin on the left side was marred with scar tissue from a long ago IED in Iraq, during his service before the Nightstalkers and then the Time Patrol. Edith was as tall, with a dancer's build, but a disproportionate nose that kept her from the ranks of potential models, not that such a career would have ever been considered. Art and research were her passions, although she'd recently added a third; the man she was standing next to.

They were standing at the corner of Elk and Duane Street in lower Manhattan, just north of City Hall and surrounded by various Federal Buildings. It was while one of those buildings was being constructed that numerous graves had been uncovered and a lost chapter in the City's history brought to light: a large burial ground for blacks during colonial times.

"The map is of the Middle Passage," Edith said as they walked inside a wall encircling the map etched in the stone laid in the ground. "The stone is from South Africa and North America, a connection between the old and New Worlds." She indicated the tall, triangular structure with an opening. "The door of return. When slaves were shipped from Africa, at the ports they were loaded from, there was a place called the *Door of No Return.* Meaning they'd never see their homeland or their families again."

"So when they died, they returned?" Eagle asked. "The opiate of religion to get one through an unbearable life?"

Edith didn't respond.

"Why were they buried here?" Eagle asked.

"Wall Street was the edge of the city for a while," Edith said. "Literally a stockade to prevent attacks from Native Americans. Freed and half freed blacks were forced to live outside the wall. A further buffer against attacks. Naturally, they needed a cemetery. Also—" she paused, then pushed on—"Trinity Church passed a regulation that no blacks could be buried inside city limits." She indicated the ground under their feet. "During the excavation of the building they found at least four-hundred-and-nineteen African bodies, but its estimated that anywhere from ten to twenty thousand were buried in this area."

"The dead are all around us," Eagle said. "Yet they still built on top of it."

"There are few places on the planet that haven't received the dead," Edith said. "Most of this area had already been built over. They modified that building's plans to accommodate this monument."

Eagle turned to face her. "Why did you bring me here?"

"You were upset about Shaka Zulu," Edith said, referring to his last mission to Southeast Africa in 1828.

"He was a brutal psychopath," Eagle said, "who murdered his own people. Yet he's probably the best known of black African leaders in history."

"But he helped you against the Aglaeca and Grendels," Edith said. "He died fighting for the human race."

Eagle shook his head sadly. "No. He fought because he loved battle. He reveled in blood. Even that of his own people. And I still don't see the connection to—"

"The thousands buried here," Edith said, "would have been completely lost to history except for a handful of people who learned of what was here and had the construction stopped. Who fought to have the country pay homage to the dead. Shaka was history. This is history."

Eagle looked at the inscription on the exterior stone of the memorial:

For all those who were lost
For all those who were stolen
For all those who were left behind
For all those who were not forgotten

Edith put her arm around Eagle. "It's easy to lose track of reality when we go to the Possibility Palace. And for you, and your teammates, who travel in time. We have to ground ourselves. This represents both the worst, slavery, and the best, hope for future generations. Remember, when you travel back in time, you're often going to the worst."

POSSIBILITY PALACE

"I saw the Shadow's timeline," Scout told Dane and Sin Fen.

"I read the debrief," Dane said.

"You saw Atlantis," Sin Fen said. "The only one left in existence that we know of."

"Are you certain?" Scout asked.

"No," Sin Fen admitted.

"Why did the Shadow destroy the other Atlantis?" Scout asked. She'd been recruited into the Nightstalkers years ago, at the not so tender age of sixteen, when they'd gone into a gated community in North Carolina to shut down a Rift. It was the team sergeant, Nada, who'd sensed there was something special about her and given her the name and it had stayed with her as she grew into a young woman. She'd transitioned with the team from Nightstalker to Time Patrol. Average height, slender, her short hair was newly dyed jet black.

"We're not certain," Sin Fen said. "But the best theory is that there was once only a single timeline. The original Atlantis. Humans advanced very far in certain technologies, especially physics. Someone opened the first Rift and in doing so, shattered the timeline."

"Into how many?" Scout pressed.

"We don't know," Sin Fen said. "If you asked Ivar, he'd say it would be an infinite number. Once permutations began, the possibilities are endless. We still don't understand the physics involved."

"But the Shadow does," Scout said.

"To an extent," Dane replied. "That's how it can open Gates and move in time and attack other timelines."

"But it can't completely control the Gates," Scout said. "It can't keep us from going into the bubbles they create in our past."

Sin Fen and Dane exchanged a glance.

"What?" Scout asked.

"We're not sure it's a flaw in the Shadow's Gates," Dane said. "We might be getting help getting into those bubbles."

"Who?" Scout asked. "The Ones Before? The Fates?"

"We don't know," Sin Fen said.

"What is the Shadow afraid of?" Scout asked. "I don't understand why it's trying to destroy us."

"We're a threat," Dane said. "The Shadow is afraid other timelines will master what they have, perhaps go beyond their technology, and attack them. They're being pre-emptive. In some cases, they're scavenging timelines and people."

Dane sat behind a bland gray desk in a room with off white walls. There were no pictures or paintings on those walls. The top of the desk was clean. A pneumatic tube ran from floor to ceiling behind him. The room could be anywhere, which was appropriate since the Possibility Palace could not only be anywhere on Earth, it could be any time.

"What does it mean that I saw the Shadow's timeline outside of the time tunnel I was returning through?" Scout asked.

Dane looked at Sin Fen to answer. He was of average height, unshaven, the stubble more white than black. He wasn't of this Earth timeline, but rather a refugee from one that had battled the Shadow and lost. He'd been worn out when he arrived, but defiant ever since joining the Time Patrol and taking command.

"You have the Sight," Sin Fen said.

"Have *you* seen the Shadow's timeline?" Scout asked.

Sin Fen nodded. "Occasionally."

"What does it mean?" Scout repeated. "Are we getting closer to stopping the Shadow? Is that why nothing's happened for a while? Have we stopped it? Did some other timeline destroy it?"

"No." Dane's voice was unequivocal. "As long as that timeline exists, the Shadow exists."

"And we're certain it still exists?" Scout asked.

"We are," Sin Fen confirmed. "But you seeing it is interesting. Perhaps the Shadow is losing some control or has problems that we don't know about. There's been unusual activity in the Space Between."

"What activity?" Scout asked.

"That's not important right now," Dane interjected.

"What about what Lara saw there?" Scout asked. "In the tubes? The girl who was her. The boy who was Lukas? Is Lara from the Shadow? Is that why you didn't invite her to this meeting?"

"Lara *is* from the Shadow," Sin Fen said, "but not *of* the Shadow."

"What the frak does that mean?" Scout demanded.

Dane answered. "We don't know. The other tubes contained Legion, clones that the Shadow uses as disposable warriors to go into other timelines. She, and Lukas, were developed in the same mode but are different. Not just warriors."

"She has the Sight," Sin Fen said. "That's a new development. We've fought Legion before. They are worthy adversaries, but one with Sight? Very dangerous."

"Lara's on our side," Scout said. "Perhaps by giving her the Sight, they gave her an awareness that allowed her to make her own choices, unlike Legion who are programmed to kill? To not participate in the eradication of other timelines?"

"'Eradication'?" Dane repeated, arching an eyebrow.

"Eagle's been teaching Lara and me," Scout said. "You know. Stuff."

"If that's true about Lara," Sin Fen said, "then she's flawed," She held up her hand to stop Scout's protest. "She thought she was in an insane asylum when she was actually in a black ops site being evaluated. We don't know how she ended up there in the first place. She escaped. Somehow, she ended up with us. We think whatever the Shadow did to her when they grew and programmed her didn't work out as they desired."

"'Grew her'?"

"She's a clone," Dane said. "Grown in a tube. And I disagree with Sin Fen on one major point. Lara might not be flawed. She might be functioning exactly as the Shadow desires in infiltrating us. Getting us to trust her."

"I trust her," Scout said. "Completely."

"I don't," Dane said.

"You don't trust anyone," Scout shot back.

Dane granted her a small smile. "True. But we do the best we can. And Lara did help the team. For now, we accept her. But we must always be aware that she might not know who she really is."

"Do any of us?" Scout said and there was no answer.

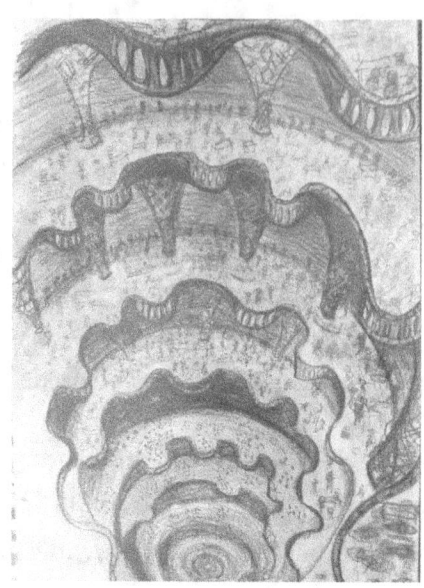

The Pit

THE TOPIC of conversation was standing on the edge of a yawning pit, peering over the railing into its depths. The vague bottom was over a mile down; the beginning of recorded history. spiral track ran counter-clockwise along the outside of the pit. It was of varying widths, depending on the importance of the spot in the timeline and the number of Time Patrol analysts assigned to that era.

The analysts sat at bland grey desks, the same as the one in Dane's office. There were no computers, phones, or electronic devices at all. Nothing that could be hacked into by the Shadow. They wrote their reports in hieroglyphics that were ancient and universal to all the agents. There were, however, lots and lots of filing cabinets stacked along the outer edge, against the stonewall. There were occasional zip lines going across and ladders here and there, going from one level to another, making direct connections between certain eras quicker than walking the spiral. Pneumatic tubes lined the walls. The analysts sat in their sector of time, experts on the history of their slice. They were constantly studying, going over their data. Because, like the art, if any form of data started to change, it portended a Shadow assault.

To Lara's right, as the spiral ascended ever so slightly, the ramp faded into a gray mist: the future that was yet to unfold. Overhead was a deep grey cloud. If that got hit by a Time Tsunami coming from below and turned black, then it would be over an instant later. All would cease to exist.

Lara wasn't watching anything in particular. She was listening. There was the faint murmur of hieroglyphic typewriters, the voices of analysts speaking in many languages, file drawers opening and closing, but she was listening beyond that. Lara was waiting for the voices in her head. She found it amusing that Sin Fen called it the Sight, when for her it was the more the voices. The ones she could hear occassionally from the Pit, from the billions of humans who'd lived and died through history. They were all part of history, whether they had a large role to play, or like most, hadn't seemed significant at all except to those who loved them.

And there were other voices that crept into her head at times. Sin Fen said they might be the Ones Before, although no one quite knew who *they* were. Or the Fates.

But the voices had been quiet for a while now, ever since coming back from the last mission. Lara closed her eyes, tuning the normal noise out. She was barely five and a half feet tall, slender. Her hair was the same color as Scout, since they'd done the coloring together. It was long enough now to cover the jigsaw of scars on her skull.

They don't trust me.

Duh. I don't trust me. But I went through that door. Faced Joey. Legion. Whatever. Whoever.

But I was in that pod. Another me. And another Lukas.

That can't be good.

What do I do if I face another me?

Lara giggled. She gripped the railing tighter.

"Lara?"

Lara opened her eyes, recognizing a real voice. "Hey, Scout. What did they decide?"

"Nothing," Scout said. "The usual nobody knows nothing."

"Dane's 'vagaries of the variables'," Lara said.

"Yeah." Scout didn't look happy. "I wonder about Sin Fen."

"What about her?"

"She's holding back some of what she knows."

Lara nodded. "Probably. Same with Dane. What's it Moms says? 'Need to know'? Apparently, we don't have it."

"We have something, though," Scout said. "Some of what Sin Fen has. The Sight."

"I wonder if I should try to Edge her," Lara mused.

"'Edge'?"

Lara shook her head. "It wouldn't work with her. She's got the same power. You probably do too." She explained. "Edging is putting something in your voice to get people to agree with you."

"How do you do it?"

Lara shrugged. "I don't know exactly. You just want to get someone to agree, and it happens."

"Weird." Scout perked up. "Wanna watch some more Buffy?"

Lara was about to agree, but then she cocked her head, listening. "Oh."

"What is it?" Scout asked.

Lara held up a hand for silence and looked down into the Pit, as if she could see where the voice was coming from. "It's Unity Hale." She was referring to the young girl she'd rescued on her last mission to Salem near the end of the witch trials.

Scout nodded, not daring to speak and interrupt. Lara closed her eyes.

"She's happy with the Indians. They respect her. Her Sight.

Her ability to heal. But—" Lara frowned. The two young women remained still for two minutes, which doesn't sound long, but time can stretch out at certain moments and this was one of them. Even the normal noise of the Pit seemed to diminish.

Then Lara was back, here, now. She opened her eyes. "She's fading."

"Unity?" Scout said. "How?"

"From reality."

Scout looked up at the grey cloud. There was a tinge of red in one spot. "A mission is coming."

"And Unity is threatened," Lara said with certainty but her mind went elsewhere: *And that means Scout's very existence because Unity is her great, great, grand, grand, however many generations back —Mother.*

METROPOLITAN MUSEUM OF ART.
NEW YORK CITY

Ivar scooted in the rolling chair across the tile floor, noting the slight sound of small pieces of broken glass underneath the wheels. Support had done a lousy job cleaning up the room after Security had shot to pieces all the computers in it. But all Ivar cared was that the computers had been replaced with top of the line models. There were still bullet holes in the whiteboard covering the walls, even the back of the only door, but that wasn't laziness on Support's part. Ivar had insisted they remain because the whiteboards held his calculations.

It hadn't occurred to him to order new boards and copy the old ones and replace them. Ivar's brain didn't work that way. The way it did work made him valuable to the Time Patrol. He was a scientist and had been recruited into the Nightstalkers during the same mission where they'd picked up Scout in North Carolina. Ivar had been working for a faculty member at the University of North

Carolina who'd cracked the Rubik's Cube of opening a Rift. The fact that during the battle to close that dimensional tear Ivar had been replicated a number of times had left him with a nagging doubt whether he really was Ivar. The original. But he was the only one in this timeline, so what did it matter?

There were two tables in the room, each holding a computer. One was connected to the government's dark web. The other wasn't connected to anything. The first was to gather information and had a cutoff switch, much like the one that could turn off the pumps at a gas station. Given the recent Zero Day attack, it was apparent the Shadow understood the Internet and its vulnerabilities. The stand-alone computer was the one on which he did his thinking and ran his calculations. Ivar was a big believer that thoughts floating around in his head were nothing. They had to be written down in order to become real, to gain substance. Even better, to be translated into a formula.

The room was six hundred feet below the Metropolitan Museum of Art, ensconced in the granite bedrock of Manhattan Island. If he went out the door he could go to the elevator to the surface or, straight ahead, to the Hub which held the Gate.

Ivar was lost in the dark web, looking. For what? He was following the advice of Edith Frobish, who, although she had a PhD, wasn't a 'real' doctor in Ivar's former professor's opinion. Ivar's instructor had considered physicists the be-all and end-all. Of course, although he'd managed to open a Rift, that had brought the Nightstalkers and the end of the professor, so maybe he hadn't been as smart as he'd thought he was. However, Ivar did grant that Edith was very, very good at research. She was as meticulous as he was, which he respected. She'd told him to stop asking the web questions. To start following bread crumbs. To keep his mind free of the questions because that would mean he'd overlook that which he wasn't looking for.

That had made a strange sort of sense to Ivar.

Anomalies, Edith has said. *Find what doesn't fit. What doesn't make sense. What's out of the ordinary.*

Few people had as much free range of the entire web as Ivar. Perhaps a half dozen people at the NSA, a couple at the CIA. That was it. He could go anywhere inside the supposedly secure firewalls of not only the United States government but others that the NSA had hacked their way into.

Thus, Ivar didn't know how he'd ended up in the communication stream of the Russian version of the Nightstalkers: their team that shut down Rifts. Which Ivar now viewed as sort of the ordinary, extraordinary Special Operations; junior league to the Time Patrol. Rifts were like baby Gates. They opened, things came through, mostly Fireflies, and they had to be shut. But they weren't a threat to the world as we know it. Or at least had not gotten to that stage.

Of course, the Russians no longer had a time patrol, having lost their HUB when the Ratnik were contaminated by Chernobyl, given that their headquarters had been right there with the reactor.

Ivar sat up straighter. The Russians were reporting . . .

Nothing. No reports at all, as if their team to deal with Rifts didn't exist.

He checked the Russian Kamiokande, part of a system of three; the other were in Japan and at Area 51, called the Can. It was a large, underground device for detecting muons. If it registered a spike in muonic activity, that indicated a Rift getting ready to open. That data stream was gone also.

He checked Japan.

Nothing.

All three Cans were off-line.

～

SIX HUNDRED FEET ABOVE IVAR, Moms pushed open a nondescript door on the south side of the Museum of Art. It was marked with AUTHORIZED PERSONNEL ONLY stenciled in faded red on a rusting sign.

"No guard?" Angus asked as they entered.

"Not here," Moms said. "We used to have one. He died."

"You know," Angus said as the door thudded shut behind them, "art hasn't been around that long. What if something happens before the art?"

They were in a dimly lit corridor with a marble floor.

"Five thousand years is represented in the Museum," Moms said. "But I went back to the beginning. At least part of the beginning, of art. Pre-history. On a mission. Cave drawings."

"Died or was killed?" Angus said, looping back to her first answer.

"Killed."

"You were breached?"

"Once." Moms turned to face him. "That was the first time I came here. With the rest of my team. We were called in to seal the breach."

"And you stayed."

"We stayed." Moms strode off, Angus a step behind.

"What happened to the first team?"

"We don't know."

"Why did you go back to cavemen time?" Angus asked.

"The Shadow was trying to wipe out the first artist. It was a key point in human development. And it might have been a cavewoman."

"Intriguing," Angus said.

They reached an intersection and instead of taking the brightly lit corridor to the right, they turned into the almost dark, narrower one to the right. A piece of yellow tape drooped across it and a sign hanging from it read:

CLOSED FOR CONSTRUCTION

Moms lifted it and Angus ducked through. They continued. The corridor transitioned from an addition to an older part of the Museum. Moms indicated the wall to the right. "This was the outer wall of the original Museum."

They arrived at an old elevator. The sign on the copper doors read:

OUT OF ORDER

"Such threatening signage, I'm quivering in me boots," Angus noted.

"It keeps out the curious and the foolish. People sometimes wander away from the exhibits."

"Indeed. It keeps away the rule followers."

Moms spared him a glance as she pushed the down button. "That's what Edith calls them."

"Told you. Smart lass."

The doors opened, revealing a freight elevator. There were no obvious floor buttons on the inside. Moms touched one marked:

FIRE DEPARTMENT USE ONLY

She kept her finger on it long enough for her print to be scanned and verified. The doors slid shut smoothly. They descended swiftly.

Angus began humming *The Girl From Ipanema*.

Moms ignored him.

The halt was quick enough that both had to flex their knees. The doors opened to a narrow brick hallway.

"Are there any other floors?" Angus asked as they got off.

"No."

"Sure?"

Moms didn't respond. They walked down the tiled corridor.

"Reminds me of the Super-Max more than a bit," Angus noted.

Moms ignored that too.

They turned right at an intersection.

Angus paused and touched the brick. "How old is this?"

"Older than the Museum," Moms said.

"A wee bit odd, don't you think? How long has this Time Patrol been in business?"

"I don't know."

Angus chuckled. "A wee bit of a conundrum in the core of that question, don't there be?"

There was finally a guard. A hard-eyed man in black combat gear, weapon to his shoulder. He didn't relax as Moms held up a badge. He was focused on Angus, recognizing a kindred spirit of the dark arts, although Moms was no slouch.

Moms indicated an eye scanner. "You're in the system but have to clock in."

"I've heard these gadgets cause brain tumors," Angus said, but he pressed his forehead against the rubber bridge and peered into the scanner. It beeped once and a light went from red to green.

Moms did the same.

Green once more and the guard lowered the weapon as a steel door at the end of the corridor opened. They passed through and the door shut behind them. Another steel door awaited. A single light bulb buzzed overhead.

"No cheery greetings with the staff?" Angus asked.

"The guards don't know what they're guarding," Moms said. "They rotate every six weeks. They understand their job. We don't want to know them and they don't want to know us."

"Aye, smart," Angus approved. He pointed up. "Explosives?"

"Too much damage. Gas."

"Deadly or incapacitating?"

"If someone got this far, deadly." Moms put her hand over a sensor. A needle popped up, taking a sample. The DNA was processed and confirmed. The far door opened.

A large cavern loomed in front of them, two hundred meters long by a hundred wide. Spotlights were focused on a ramp leading up to a Gate. Which was a dark rectangle, composed of blackness that sucked the light in.

Moms didn't hesitate. Her long legs ate up the distance and she strode toward the ramp. Angus followed.

Moms abruptly stopped at the base of the ramp and faced Angus. "It bothers me that you don't believe you have a future."

"No one in the Super-Max does," Angus said.

"You're not there anymore," Moms said. "Add to it that you don't believe your Choice was really a Choice. That means your motivation for joining the team is flimsy."

Angus raised a bushy eyebrow, but he nodded. "I get your reasoning."

"Even though we go on missions alone, we're still a team. There have been times when team members have had to help each other. Across time. Even sacrifice their lives."

"And you're Moms."

"I am."

They locked eyes for several seconds. Angus took a step back. "What do you want to know, Moms?"

"Whether we can count on you, Angus?"

"You've been through enough to know words canna suffice," Angus said. "It's only when the pot is in the fire that we'll know for certain."

Moms pointed. "You go through the Gate at the top of the ramp and you're part of the team."

"Aye."

"Once we get a mission tasking, the date, and the years, things move quickly. We won't have time to think about things. We have to act. The fact Cleopatra's Needle is flickering in my existence, not yours, means *I'm* flickering. Because I've traveled in time and have some sort of connection to the multiverse that you don't. Yet. A mission is imminent."

Angus didn't say anything.

"When some of us were the Nightstalkers," Moms said, "we had a woman who gave us our missions. Ms. Jones. She used to ask each new team member the same thing after she gave them a short spiel."

"And that be?"

"She called it 'why we're here'."

Angus folded his arms and waited.

"We're here," Moms said, pointing to the Gate, "because the best of intentions can go horribly wrong. And the worst of intentions can achieve exactly what it sets out to do. The Shadow has the worst of intentions: to destroy our timeline, among others. If it can change six events in our history, cause six Cascades, that will form a time tsunami that will wipe us out of our existence. We, the Time Patrol, are the last line of defense against that. We accept there are things out there—not just the Shadow, but monsters its created such as kraken and Grendels, and humans who fight for it like Legion and Spartan mercenaries, that try to kill us. There are others, such as the Ones Before, the Fates, and more—beyond our knowledge and understanding. Mankind must be guarded against all threats and even those who appear to help.

"You were SAS early in your career," Moms continued. "Who Dares Wins. You know what it's like to man the walls in the middle of the night." She pointed up. "The walls between all those innocents out there who lay their heads down on their pillows every evening, troubled by thoughts of such things as mortgages, or their pet is sick, or their child is failing in school. The normal things people should worry about. We worry about far graver issues. The very existence of all we know." She locked eyes once more. "Can you live with that?"

"Aye."

"You need to get to work and read the briefing book as soon as we get there."

"Aye."

Moms turned and walked up the ramp. She didn't hesitate, stepping into the Gate and snapping out of this time and place.

Angus followed.

He was whistling Colonel Bogey's March as he stepped through, more commonly known as the theme from *The Bridge of the River Kwai.*

POSSIBILITY PALACE

The pneumatic tube behind Dane delivered a scroll with a resounding thump.

A special sound, because the paper was a unique weight, extra thick, and only used for mission taskings.

Dane opened the tube and retrieved the scroll. He placed it on his table and unrolled it.

22 September: 1862—White House, Washington D.C.

1692—SALEM, MASSACHUSETTS
1823—MANCHESTER, NEW YORK STATE
1776—MANHATTAN. NEW YORK CITY
1948: TEMPLEHOFF AIRFIELD, WEST BERLIN
1947—AREA 51, NEVADA

Dane ran his finger over Area 51. He knew the significance of the place. And the year.

The door to his office opened without a knock. Sin Fen entered. He turned the scroll around and slid it toward her. She leaned over the desk and read. Then sat down.

"Salem again," she said. "Same year. But a month earlier than Hallows Eve. That's intriguing."

"The Shadow might be after Scout's ancestor again," Dane

said. "Unity Hale. Persistent bastards. Kill her *before* Lara saved her on the last mission."

"That makes the agent assignment easy," Sin Fen said. "Be grateful for small blessings. Lara goes to Salem. Again."

"Fine." Dane agreed. "The analysts are delivering their packets to Edith's office. We'll have the framework for the missions."

Sin Fen turned her head as if she heard something. "Moms is here. With the new man, Angus. Edith and Eagle are close by. They'll be here soon."

"What do you think of Angus?" Dane said. "Since Frasier is no longer with us, we're not going to get the usual psych eval on the new recruit."

"You have to wonder how accurate Frasier's evals were given how he ended."

Dane nodded. "Good point. But Hannah from the Cellar insisted we have evals. Since she helps fund the Patrol in this time-line, we have to play along.

"Angus may be new to the Time Patrol," Sin Fen said, "but he's got more experience than anyone else on the team. He could be our new Nada. The glue that binds that team."

"I thought Moms was doing that," Dane said.

"Moms leads," Sin Fen said. "She's mission focused. The team needs someone people oriented. Eagle is doing the best he can, but he's . . ." She trailed off.

"Distracted by Edith?" Dane asked. "I'm concerned about the relationships. The two of them. And Roland and Neeley."

"Scout and Lara are tight," Sin Fen said. "In their own way. They share the Sight. We cannot control human nature, Eric."

Dane looked at her. "You haven't called me that in a long time."

Sin Fen shifted topics. "Ivar informs me all three Cans have gone off-line."

Dane nodded. "I know. I've made inquiries to Japan and

Russia. Area 51 has been evacuated. The Nightstalkers are on alert."

"I have a feeling it isn't coincidence this is happening at the exact moment we have a mission."

"I agree," Dane said. "I'm going to send Ivar and Angus out there to find out what's going on."

AN ISLAND OFF THE COAST OF PUERTO RICO

They'd just finished making love on the beach; a daring feat for Roland. Not the making love part, but doing it in the open. He'd had a difficult time getting into it, fearing perhaps a sniper in the treeline or a drone flying overhead with a Hellfire missile, but eventually Neeley's wiles had made him forget about security for a brief, wonderful interlude. They lay next to each other, naked, sweat-covered, sand stuck on various parts of their bodies, breathing hard.

"Wow," Roland managed.

"Wow what?" Neeley murmured, eyes half-closed, one hand lightly stroking his chest.

"Just wow."

Neeley laughed. "Wow back at you."

Then their satellite phones hidden somewhere in the piles of clothes sounded the same ringtone in concert:

Lawyers, Guns and Money.

METROPOLITAN MUSEUM OF ART.
NEW YORK CITY

As Eagle and Edith reached the intersection far below the Museum, they met Ivar who had a binder tucked under his arm and a worried look on his face. Thus, all three phones sounded at once.

Lawyers, Guns and Money.

POSSIBILITY PALACE

"No!" Lara yelled at the television as Buffy threw herself into the portal to seal it and save the world. She scrambled off the old, beat up couch and grabbed the DVD box set, checking. "But there's another season!"

They were in the team room in the Possibility Palace, which mimicked but didn't quite succeed in matching the old team room at the Ranch near Area 51. Both were keeping at bay what they knew was pending: a mission.

Scout hit the pause button. "Look." She pointed at the tombstone that was displayed.

BUFFY ANNE SUMMERS

1981-2001

BELOVED SISTER

DEVOTED FRIEND

SHE SAVED THE WORLD

A LOT

"But she'll be back, right?" Lara asked as she opened up the first DVD for season seven. She ejected the current disc and inserted it.

"Of course," Scout said. "You see—"

Their phones went off.

Lawyers, Guns and Money.

"Frak," Lara said. "Now I have to wait to find out how."

"I can tell you," Scout said.

"Nope," Lara replied. "It can wait until we get back."

"Optimism," Scout said. "I like it."

THE MISSION BRIEFING

Ivar had the binder open and was studying the data he'd intercepted; rather, the lack of data. He was dressed the same, which meant he wasn't going on a mission, unless, like last time, it was in the present. Or the near present. Across from him, Angus had the Nightstalker and Time Patrol missions' binder and was scanning the pages, flipping through as if he was barely reading.

They both looked up as the door to the prep area opened and Scout entered. She was attired in Colonial garb: petticoat, gown and kerchief on her head. She pulled at the gown, irritated by the stays underneath.

"Definitely no hot showers," Scout complained. She looked at the two of them. "You weren't tabbed to get kitted out?"

"Nope," Ivar said.

Angus didn't answer the obvious.

"Lucky you," Scout said.

"Do you often take a hot shower while on mission?" Angus asked.

"It's a metaphor," Scout said.

"Ah," Angus said. He paused, then asked. "For what, exactly, lass?"

"A time when everyone stinks and the clothes for women are uncomfortable," Scout said.

"Isn't that pretty much all of history?" Angus asked.

"Yeah," Scout said, slumping down in a chair. "But 1969 was cool. Except for the guy who tried to kill me."

"Read about that," Angus said, tapping the binder. "You did right smart there. And then."

Neeley was next, in drab grey pants and shirt. She had a tattered black coat smeared with coal dust folded over one arm. She tossed it over the back of a chair and sat down. "It's got to be in the last hundred years or so, right?"

Ivar shrugged. "Eagle's the expert on that."

"Better than this," Scout said.

"You look nice," Neeley said. "It's becoming of you."

"Wanna switch?" Scout said. "It's squeezing me like a vice. Why do women put up with crap like this?"

"Try high heels sometimes," Neeley said.

"No, thanks."

Eagle came in, wearing clothes that were definitely from an earlier period. Dark cotton pants, a white shirt, and black vest. Clean and functional. Before either Scout or Ivar could comment, he gave his best guess as to his time destination. "Mid nineteenth century." He looked at Neeley. "Mid twentieth." Scout: "Colonial era, if you're going to North America." Then Ivar. "Isn't that what you were wearing earlier?"

Ivar nodded. "Something's come up. I don't think—" he was cut off as Lara arrived. Wearing the exact same outfit, she'd been equipped with for the Hallows Eve mission.

"Well, duh," Scout said.

"Maybe I did it wrong the first time," Lara said.

"It's a time, not a place," Eagle said. "You could be going somewhere else. And it could be fifty years or so either way. Fashions didn't change as fast back then."

Lara shook her head. "No. I heard Unity. She's in trouble. I'm going to help her."

Further discussion was interrupted by Dane and Sin Fen entering the briefing room.

"Edith is still putting together the mission brief and uploads," Dane said, then he realized they were short two. "And we're still equipping. So."

Lara jumped into the void. "I'm going back to Salem, right?"

Dane hesitated, then nodded. "Yes."

Before more questions, Roland entered, brown cloth pants and a checkered shirt. Moms was last, even though she had the most modern appearing outfit. Tan slacks, sensible shoes, and a white blouse with tan blazer. Professional garb from the previous century.

"The lad and I aren't part of the fun?" Angus asked.

Dane shook his head. "Ivar has learned something is happening at Area 51. The two of you are going there. I want you to take care of him."

"And who will be taking care of me?" Angus asked.

Dane ignored the question.

Angus was disappointed, but didn't voice any further complaints as Edith came in, pushing a cart through the door. There were weapons on it along with the briefing binder and before Roland could inspect the armament, Dane waved everyone into a seat and went to the whiteboard. He uncapped a marker and wrote:

22 SEPTEMBER

"The Equinox," Eagle immediately said.

Roland asked the question several of them were thinking. "What's the Equinox?"

Edith and Eagle exchanged a glance, both willing to let the other answer, but Eagle gave her a slight nod to proceed.

"Technically," Edith said, "the equinox is the moment when the plane of the Earth's equator passes through the center of the Sun. It happens twice a year. Spring and Fall."

Roland was confused. "'Passes through the sun'?"

Eagle clarified. "When the sun is directly over the equator."

"Okay," Roland said, without much confirmation that he actually understood.

Edith tried a different approach. "It's when daylight and night-time are equal. The sun rises due east and sets due west of the equator."

Roland understood that because map reading and land navigation had been beaten to him in many Army courses over the years.

Moms was looking at Dane, waiting for him to give them the first of the mission years now that they had the date, but he didn't volunteer information.

"Hey," Angus said. "That date's in here." He tapped the Time Patrol briefing folder, which also contained the Nightstalker history." He flipped through and found it. "That's the day the first Rift opened. 1947."

"You remember that?" Ivar asked. "You were turning the pages so fast, I didn't even think you were reading."

Angus tapped the side of his head. "There's more in here than a happy-go-lucky free spirit from the highlands, lad. My mother always thought me a wee bit odd."

Dane confirmed it. "Yes. We're going to the Nightstalker's origins." He wrote on the board:

AREA 51. 1947.

He pointed the marker at Moms. "That's yours."

"The Nightstalkers were pulled together that day and closed the first Rift," Moms said. "Is the Shadow going to try to keep it open?"

"We don't know," Dane said. "But Ivar has learned the Russian and Japanese Super-Kamiokandes have gone quiet. There might be some connection."

"What about our Can?" Eagle asked.

"Also off line and no word from the duty crew," Dane said. "As a precaution, Area 51 has been evacuated."

"That's not good," Moms understated.

"It is not," Dane agreed.

"The Nightstalkers?" Moms asked.

"On alert, but we're holding off on sending them in until Angus and Ivar arrive," Dane said, "since this appears linked to our operation. It's the same place as your mission," he added to Moms. "Remember that the Demon Core was used to open that first Rift by the Odessa team. It, and Odessa, went through the first Rift."

"Will I be able to take in the gear to get containment?" Moms asked, without much hope.

"Negative," Dane said. "Too advanced. Remember, the first Rift was shut down with what they had on hand."

"A lot of people died doing that," Moms pointed out.

"Try not to be one of them," Dane said.

"That's the team spirit," Angus said.

Sin Fen spoke for the first time. "I was recently in the Space Between. Amelia Earhart says there's been considerable Valkyrie activity regarding Rifts. They're infiltrating information about how to open Rifts into timelines."

"Is that what happened in 1947?" Moms asked.

"There's no indication of that," Sin Fen said, "but it's a possibility."

"Actually," Dane said, "we believe that's Roland's mission." He grabbed a Naga spear off the cart and tossed it to Roland who happily caught it.

Dane wrote:

MANCHESTER, NEW YORK. 1823

"You've got to be kidding me," Moms said, distracted from her own assignment as she recognized the date and location.

Roland was confused. "What? What happened there? Then?"

Moms, who had done a mission regarding Mormons before on Nine-Eleven and had a lineage in the religion, answered: "That's where and when Joseph Smith, the father of Mormonism, claims to have found the gold plates which are the source of the Book of Mormon."

"We think there *are* actual gold plates," Dane said. "But they're from the Shadow. And among other things on them, some of which led Joseph Smith to write the Book of Mormon, there's information on how to open a Rift."

"Over a century too soon," Ivar noted. "No one in 1823 will understand it."

"Yes," Sin Fen agreed, "but if those plates don't disappear, like they did according to Mormon history, somebody earlier than the scientists at Area 51 could get information that might allow them to open a Rift before 1947."

"The understanding of the physics involved in opening a Rift," Ivar said, "has larger ramifications. The entire field would be advanced if that got out."

"Indeed," Dane said. "Which means that all the threads of our history wrapped around physics will be changed, such as the development of the atomic bomb. Think what happens if Germany develops it first in the 1930s?"

Roland was a few steps behind. "What do you mean disappeared? Gold plates?"

Moms explained. "Joseph Smith said an angel appeared to him and led him to a buried chest containing gold plates that had strange writing on them. We know that people tend to think Valkyries are angels. Smith called the angel who visited him Moroni."

Roland was now focused on only one thing. He held up the Naga spear. "I'm gonna fight Valkyries?"

"Don't be so enthusiastic," Neeley muttered.

"Likely," Sin Fen said.

"Cool," Roland said. "And I what, blow up these plates?"

"You'll figure it out," Dane said with more confidence than he felt.

"No problem," Roland said. He looked at the cart and asked Edith. "Any demo?"

"No," Edith said, squashing his dream. "You have to make do with what you find in the era."

Roland was already headed down that line of thought. "Yeah. There's gunpowder and—"

Dane cut him off. "Okay. Next." He wrote:

SALEM. 1692

Lara was nodding. "That's the day they hanged eight people." She pointed at her head. Then frowned. "I've seen it. Wait. I'm supposed to make sure those people hang?"

"We don't know what the Shadow has planned on any of these missions," Dane said. "You have to be open to all possibilities. We've seen missions that appeared straight-forward turn into something else. Right, Roland?"

Roland's explosives train derailed for the moment. "Yes, sir."

"The threat is against Unity Hale," Lara said. "I sense it. And just before I came back from the last mission, she showed me her memory of those eight people hanging from the gallows."

"It's likely," Dane allowed, "that it is about Unity Hale. She is a distant descendent of the original seers of Atlantis. As is Scout."

"A witch," Lara said. "I suppose I'm a different sort of witch."

"I'm a witch also," Sin Fen said. "We prefer to be called seers. We have the sight. But there's something else that might be nothing or might be important about some of these missions that we have the analysts digging into. The name. Hale. You've got Unity Hale in Salem in 1692 and--" she turned to Dane.

Dane wrote on the board:

NEW YORK CITY. 1776.

"Scout. This is you and involves a Hale." He indicated for Edith to elaborate on the mission.

"Nathan Hale was hanged on 22 September, 1776," Edith said. "He'd been on a spying mission for General Washington when he was caught and executed."

"I don't like it," Scout immediately said. She tapped Lara. "We're both supposed to let people get hung, hanged or whatever the hell is the right word?"

"Things get hung," Eagle said, "people get hanged."

"Great," Lara muttered.

"Again," Dane said, with forced patience, "we don't know what exactly the Shadow has planned to disrupt our history."

"Is Nathan Hale related to Unity Hale?" Scout asked. "Which, I guess, is asking if he's related to me?"

"That's what we're looking into," Edith said. "It's probably just a coincidence. It's a common enough name."

"Hey," Roland said, as something he'd been taught sparked. "He's the guy who said he had but one life to live or give, right?"

"According to some of the accounts of the event," Eagle said.

Edith had her own literary addition: "What he said was based on the play *Cato* written by Joseph Addison in 1712. Hale was well educated and attended Yale, so he was probably familiar with it. '*How beautiful is death, when earned by virtue. Who would not be that youth? What pity it is that we can die but once to serve our country*'."

Angus snorted. "Written by someone who hasn't danced with death. There's no beauty or virtue to it. Make the other lad die for *his* country is my rule."

"You'll have Hale's background and what is known of the event in your download," Edith told Scout.

Dane wrote on the board:

WASHINGTON D.C. 1862

"Eagle. This is yours. The day on which Lincoln announces the Emancipation Proclamation. It was announced then but wouldn't go into effective until 1 January, 1863. He used the Battle of Antietam as the impetus to publicly announce it."

"17 September was the bloodiest day in American history," Eagle said. "It wasn't a victory, but it wasn't a defeat."

"The Emancipation Proclamation is in here too," Angus said, tapping the book. "Fellow named Doc went on a mission to 1776 in Philadelphia. And Moms, you—"

She cut him off. "Yes, I was at Monticello in 1826, when Sally Hemings had to decide whether to reveal the original Declaration of Emancipation written by Jefferson in 1776 that Doc managed to get them to postpone in order to make sure the Declaration of Independence was passed."

"Hard choice," Angus said. He indicated one of the names

carved into the top of the table they sat around: *DOC*. "I'm sorry for your lost teammate."

"He sacrificed himself," Moms said, "on the Valentines Day mission, making sure we all made it out of Chicago. He stayed behind with a bomb. That's why even though we're going alone on our missions, we still need to be a team."

"Aye," Angus said. "It was a brave sacrifice the lad made." He nodded at Moms, taking the not so subtle jabs in stride.

Eagle cut in. "Nothing specific about what the Shadow might want to change on that day other than possibly stopping Lincoln from issuing the Emancipation Proclamation?"

Dane shook his head. "But it's likely you get to meet your second president."

"All right," Eagle said, accepting the 'vagaries of the variables'. He indicated one of the items hanging on the team room wall. "Can I take the Badge of Military Merit from Washington with me?"

"Certainly," Edith said. "It predates the mission."

Eagle was thinking through the ramifications. "Moms, you said that Jefferson was expecting you in 1826, right?"

Moms nodded. "Doc had told him in 1776 to expect a visitor fifty years later. Given we were both with Jefferson on the same mission, it made sense."

"And Jefferson started the Book of Truths," Eagle said. "Right?"

"Correct," Moms said, remembering their Book of Truths mission as Nightstalkers, which seemed eons ago.

"That means Lincoln has access to the Book," Eagle said. "That might make things easier in talking to him. Still." He thought for a moment. "If I have to meet Lincoln it might be difficult given the status of my people at the time."

"You'll make it work," Dane said.

Edith spoke: "There was a lot of maneuvering and political

implications behind the Proclamation. It will be in your download."

"Thank you," Eagle said.

Dane addressed the team. "As always. Don't get tunnel vision. The Shadow has thrown the unexpected at us before."

"And me?" Neeley said. "What shouldn't I expect?"

Dane wrote:

BERLIN. 1948.

Edith Frobish detailed the mission. "On 24 June 1948, the Soviet Union blockaded all rail, road and water access to West Berlin which was occupied by French, British and American troops. It was an effort to get them to withdraw and bring all of Berlin into Soviet controlled East Germany. The British and Americans responded with an airlift of critical supplies beginning on 26 June.

"You need to understand," Edith continued, "that this was only three years after the end of World War II. Most of the supplies were going to the defeated Germans. The impetus for the airlift was geopolitical, to keep the Soviet Union in check. However, to maintain it as long as they did was fraught with the possibility of losing the support of the people of the United States and Great Britain who didn't see the point of so much effort being expended to assist a former enemy; especially one that had enacted such evil.

"A pilot began dropping candy to the children of Berlin from his plane as he came in to land at Templehoff. He became known as the Candy Bomber. Other pilots followed suit and it became very popular back in the States. That small act by one pilot of dropping candy, expanded and caught the attention of the people. It was a major propaganda coup. The entire airlift was one of American's greatest moments."

The words had come out in a rush and they were all looking at her by the time she was done.

Edith blushed. "I'm sorry. It's not often that I find historical events that are so . . ." She was at a momentary loss.

"Uplifting?" Angus said.

Neeley hadn't said anything about her assignment.

Roland leaned close to her. "You okay?"

"Can someone else take Berlin?" Neeley asked, without much hope.

"We have reasons for each assignment," Dane said. "You're the perfect fit for this mission. You've lived in Berlin, albeit a bit later. And you speak German with a Berliner accent."

Roland was surprised. "You lived in Berlin? You speak German?"

"It was a long time ago," Neeley said. "What happened on 22 September?"

Edith's confidence faded slightly. "We haven't found anything special. We're still digging, but it seems like a relatively ordinary day in an extraordinary operation."

Sin Fen spoke up. "The Airlift was the most critical flash point in escalating tensions between east and west early in the Cold War. For a long time, the world stood on the brink of World War III and Berlin was the tinderbox that could ignite it. Although we've found nothing of significance occurring in Berlin on 22 September 1948, we know that the Shadow is planning something that would change history."

"How will I know what to look for?" Neeley asked.

"Trust what you have in the download," Dane said, "and your instincts."

"I have a question on that," Neeley said. "I know I'm relatively new to the team, but how exactly are we going where we need to go at the time we need to go there, if the Shadow is the one opening up the Gate and the bubble?"

"We don't know," Dane said. "We suspect either the Ones Before or the Fates allow us to slip an agent into the bubble and become part of the day. The good news is that wherever you end up, it's damn close or right on top of whatever the Shadow is going to change."

"Are we being played?" Angus asked, tapping the binder. "If these Fates or Ones Before really want to help, why don't they just stop the Shadow? Why do they need us?"

"We don't know," Dane said. "Perhaps they're not powerful enough."

Moms turned to Angus. "Several of us have run into the Fates on our missions. They can help but they seem bound by some sort of code. Or perhaps their power is limited."

"According to this," Angus said, "these Fates can bring a person back to life. Happened during the Vicksburg mission. That's pretty powerful."

"Do you remember everything you read?" Ivar asked.

"A wee bit," Angus said.

Dane spread his hands. "I've already admitted our ignorance. We know what we have to do and we do it. We're trying to learn more. That's one of the reasons you're going with Ivar to Area 51. You're to check on the Can."

"What's the connection to this mission?" Moms asked.

"That's why I'm sending them," Dane said. "To find out if there is one."

"Is there anything more?" Moms asked.

"Those are the missions," Dane said.

"You all have your Naga daggers, correct?" Moms asked.

Angus held up a hand. "Not equipped here."

Edith reached into her cart and produced one of the black knives made of the special metal that could cut through Valkyrie armor.

"What other weapons?" Roland asked, always ready to load up.

"Edith will give them to you once we're done with the briefing," Dane said. He looked to Moms.

"We should have a naming ceremony for Angus," Moms said, "but we need to get uploaded and Ivar and Angus have a trip to make." She stood. "Let's finish gearing up, receive our downloads and get going."

As they left the briefing room to get their downloads, Edith surreptitiously slipped something small into Eagle's hand.

THE MISSIONS PHASE I

"The time is now near at hand which must probably determine whether Americans are to be freemen or slaves."
George Washington address to the Continental Army,
27 August 1776, just prior to the Battle of Long Island.
They lost.

NEW YORK CITY. 22 September 1776

Scout WASN'T THERE, and then she was there, but she'd sort of always been there. She was growing weary of going to places that didn't have hot, running water. She also didn't like the outfit she was wearing, although she did fit in with the two other serving women and the cook crowded into the kitchen. Scout kept a steady hand on the tray she was holding as she got oriented.

At least there wasn't a Legion waiting to slice her up as there had been on her previous mission. An old, grizzled black woman was working a large wood stove covered with sizzling pans. Scout smelled burning wood, bacon and strong coffee and there was the murmur of English voices coming through one of the two doors in the kitchen. The first light of dawn was tinting the eastern horizon through the narrow, glazed window to the right of the fireplace.

"Get moving, girl, or I'll whack you one," one of the other servingwomen snapped. She was dressed like Scout but older, with the aura of *'I'm one rung on the ladder above you'*. "Stop your daydreaming, girl." She waved a wooden spoon with intent, indicating her threat was not idle.

The ladder was probably lodged deep in the pit of indentured servitude, but it was in a different realm from the cook as Edith's download informed Scout that at this moment, New York City had more slaves than any other place in the country, except Charleston, South Carolina.

It is 1776 A.D. The world's population is a little over 900 million, of which 3.6 million are part of the fledgling United States; Thomas Paine publishes Common Sense; *; the Illuminati is formally founded in Bavaria; angry New Yorkers cover a statue of King George III with graffiti and then topple it; Edward Gibbons publishes* The History of the Decline and Fall of the Roman Empire; *the Liberty Bell rings; near the end of the year, King George makes a speech to Parliament and says all isn't going as well as one would like in the war with the unruly colonists but there was a light at the end of the tunnel; the western frontier, where Native Americans and encroaching white settlers are killing each other with unbridled savagery over land, is only a few hundred miles to the west, in exotic lands called Ohio and Kentucky; just a few weeks earlier, George Washington is defeated in what history would record as the largest battle of the Revolution at the Battle of Long Island; the population of New York City is twenty-five thousand, second only to Philadelphia.*

Scout knew she was in New York, Manhattan more particularly, but she accessed the download to narrow it down to determine where exactly Nathan Hale was on the morning of 22 September 1776; the day of his death.

The answer was there: she was in the Beekman House overlooking Turtle Bay on the East River, which present day, her present day, would be around 50th Street and First Avenue, but was now north of city limits and in the gentrified countryside. There was indeed a bay below the bluff on which the house stood. It was crowded with the masts of sailing ships. Data poured in before Scout could shut it down: the bay had been filled in after the Civil War and the land on which this house stood had been leveled. In Scout's time the United Nations would be built here, over the site where a row of slaughterhouses that would exist for over a century after this.

Since the British had crossed over from Long Island on the 15th of September, just eight days ago, General William Howe, their commander, had established his headquarters in the house. His brother, Admiral Richard Howe, commanding the British naval forces, stayed here when he wasn't on board ship.

"Move! They don't like waiting!" The woman scolding Scout was red-faced, overweight and appeared ready for a coronary which, given the amount of bacon and sausage sizzling, was likely. She accompanied the words with a smack of the spoon on the top of Scout's head, who resisted the impulse to dump the tray on the woman's head.

Scout went with the prod and carried the tray through the door to the dining room. A dozen men in scarlet uniforms sat around a long table. There was a fireplace with a black marble mantel inscribed with elaborate carvings. Paintings covering most of the walls that Scout supposed were valuable and impressive but looked like a bunch of old farts sitting around waiting to get painted. There were tall columns that seemed to serve no purpose except decoration. The windows on one side of the room looked out over Turtle Bay and the East River, which was crowded with British ships of the line.

One of the officers snapped his fingers at Scout. "Here, girl."

Scout realized she was carrying a platter of the bacon and sausage. She hurried over. Uncertain of the protocol and not wishing to dig through the layers of Edith's extensive download, Scout simply held it out toward the man to help himself.

He stared at her in surprise, then laughed. "Ah, you colonials. Lost all traces of civilization in this God-forsaken place. We might as well be eating off the floor. Lord knows why we're trying to keep you in the Empire."

"Easy, Captain Montresor," the older man at the head of the table said. Despite only having a painting to draw on in the download, Scout recognized him as General Howe. He appeared old and tired compared to the painting but the brush took away a dozen years at least. Scout understood the look in the General's eyes: he'd seen too much death and took too much responsibility for it. Nada had had the same in his eyes and Scout felt the twinge of loss for her old friend.

The download informed Scout that the previous summer General Howe led the attack on Bunker Hill outside Boston, where the British had finally prevailed on their third frontal assault but at the horrendous cost of a thousand casualties. The river of blood of his soldiers had taken something out of the general, who'd assumed command of all British troops in North America shortly afterward. According to Edith's data, General Howe would hereafter tend to be conservative in his strategies, trying to avoid another such bloody victory. That tentativeness would lead a lack of initiative that eventually doomed the British cause.

"Has the prisoner been fed?" General Howe asked Scout. More particular and pertinent to the mission, according to the download, Howe had questioned Hale the previous evening, but learned little, since Hale knew little.

A burly, red-faced man in scarlet fringed with green, halfway down the table, spoke up as he poured from a crystal decanter. "No sense feeding him, General. He won't be needing it. Waste of food."

"I believe not, sir," Scout said, having no clue as to Hale's condition.

"Take him some sustenance," Howe ordered. He glanced at the man who had commented. "It's early in the day to be partaking, Major Rogers, is it not?"

Robert Rogers shrugged, but finished pouring. "Whatever you say, General. The prospect of pending death makes me thirsty and desirous of living life to its fullest."

Howe pointed at the decanter. "Take that with you, girl," he ordered Scout. "The prisoner might desire some."

"Yes, sir." Scout balanced the tray with one hand and leaned between Rogers and the officer next to him and grabbed the decanter. She felt a hand push into her petticoat from behind and for the first time was grateful for the multiple layers as Rogers copped a feel of cloth. She resisted her impulse to do serious harm to the man but this mission was already testing her patience.

"Haven't seen you before," Rogers whispered. "I'll have to chat with you later."

Scout extracted herself from his pawing and hurried out of the room.

"Where you going, girl?" the older woman demanded as Scout threw some food on a plate and headed for the door with the bottle.

"The General ordered me to feed the prisoner."

"Ah." The woman nodded. "Poor lad. Tell him to drink all the spirits. It'll help with what's coming." She lowered her voice. "And better he get it than those in there," she nodded toward the kitchen.

Given there were two doors in the kitchen, Scout headed for

the other one. There was no floor plan of the building in the download, just a lot of blather about the nature of the architecture, that it was made of thick wooden planks and brick, two stories tall with a basement and topped with a Dutch-style hipped roof. *Whatever the hell that was*, Scout thought as she passed down a narrow hall. And, given Edith loaded it, a lot about the artwork. *Useful stuff, Edith, useful stuff.*

A tidbit was important though. The Beekman House had the first greenhouse in North America that grew orange trees and Nathan Hale was being held in it. An exterior door on the first floor of the main house was propped open to the cool early September air and Scout exited. She had only a couple of drawings of the exterior of the house in the download and none of them quite agreed and they didn't show where the greenhouse was but given the river was in the paintings, the front of the house faced south on the bluff overlooking the cove, and since the river was ahead, she turned left and went to the back.

A single guard dressed in scarlet with white cross belts stood his post outside the door to the greenhouse. He had the butt of his musket cupped in one hand, the barrel resting along his right side, bayonet poking up over shoulder. It didn't look like the best ready-for-action stance Scout had ever seen, but it was kind of cute.

Scout walked up to him, plate in one hand, decanter in the other. "The General wanted me to give the prisoner some sustenance."

Scout was beginning to suspect Edith had added some vocabulary in the language portion of the download as if English wasn't her primary tongue and for a moment Scout resented the implication but then realized it was just Edith being Edith.

The redcoat pulled open the door and indicated for her to enter. The interior was crowded with greenery and it took Scout a moment to spot Nathan Hale seated cross-legged on the ground with his back to a small orange tree. He had a wooden board across his lap and was writing on a piece of parchment with a quill pen.

Scout was taken aback with how young he appeared. She knew from the download that he was only twenty-one, but there are those who've lived a lot by that age and looked it and those who still had that aura of youth and innocence. Hale fell into the latter camp.

She hated these missions.

He was so focused on what he was writing that he didn't look up as she approached. Scout halted a few steps away and waited for him to acknowledge her presence. She took the opportunity to look around. It *was* a greenhouse and she wondered why he hadn't broken some glass during the night and escaped?

Which made her wonder if this was going to be like Mac's Sir Walter Raleigh/Black Tuesday mission where there had been conspirators plotting to help the nobleman escape the executioner's blade. She wasn't sure if she could stop such an attempt after seeing Hale.

He must have smelled the food because he paused and looked up. There were dark circles under his eyes from a sleepless night. "Yes?"

"Food, sir. And drink."

Hale shook his head. "I desire neither." His voice was barely above a whisper and the look in his eyes was one of dazed shock, which was understandable. "I requested a Bible last night but one has not been provided. But they send me spirits? To dull my wits, I suppose."

"A little can't hurt," Scout said, although she had no idea if it would do any good for the condemned man to get a buzz on.

She put the plate and decanter down next to the inkwell on the ground. She glanced over her shoulder but the guard had closed the door behind her. She knelt in front of him. He looked up, their eyes meeting.

"Has anyone contacted you?" Scout asked.

Hale was confused. "Who? About what?"

Scout focused her voice. "Escape."

"Are you with us?" Hale asked.

"I am a friend."

"Were you sent?"

"In a manner of speaking," Scout said.

Hale shook his head. "No. You aren't a friend. You're another of Major Rogers' tricks. He pretended he was with the cause in the tavern yesterday. He took me into his confidence. Then betrayed me. That man has no honor. He's a drunken lout."

A man spoke from behind. "Careful with the insults now."

Scout jumped to her feet and spun about, hand going for the dagger hidden in a sheath inside her petticoat. She didn't draw it though because Major Robert Rogers was standing there with a pistol in his hand.

"I didn't think you were just a serving girl," Rogers said, "and your words to the prisoner prove I am right. I think we should enjoy seeing two hanged today."

Some things change; some don't.

> *"When change cometh, she will bring peace at her back.*
> *She will not bend to your will; you bend to hers."*
> Adriana Mather. *How to Hang a Witch*

SALEM, MASSACHUSETTS. 22 September 1692

Laura wasn't there, and then she was there, but she'd sort of always been there. It was the best way to explain how she arrived, becoming part of her current time and place without fanfare or excitement among those around her, because there wasn't anyone around her.

Except, once more, for Pandora, who was very aware of her sudden arrival out of time.

"You again," the 'goddess' complained.

"Have we met?" Lara said.

Pandora's tall frame was wrapped in a white robe. Her hair was jet black with a single streak of silver that started above her left eye and flowed over her scalp down to her back. She held a Naga staff, with the seven-headed snake pommel on the ground, the sharp end pointing up.

"Are you trying to be amusing?" Pandora asked.

They were in a moonlit clearing in the forest, the leaves just beginning to turn with the season. Lara recognized it from her previous mission.

"Nope," Lara said. "I never joke."

"I miss Scout," Pandora said. She drummed her fingers on the haft of the Naga staff. "Hmm. What year did she go to? Not Berlin. Awful city, especially in that year. Lincoln? No. That would be Eagle. He's already met Washington and the issue would be near to his heart. But I would have thought this mission not only near to Scout's heart, but her very existence. And you're the one they trusted with it?"

"We gotta do what we gotta do," Lara said as she headed for the path toward the village. Her eyes were adjusting and she was able to see in the dark, almost as if she were using night vision goggles. A byproduct of the 'Sight'.

Pandora belatedly hurried to keep up. "Do you know who you are? What you are? I've learned some things since we last met."

Lara ducked and the blade of Pandora's Naga staff harmlessly sliced air above her. Lara did a leg sweep, knocking Pandora's feet out from under her before she'd finished the attempt to behead her. Pandora fell to the ground and Lara was on top of her, Naga dagger at the goddess' throat.

It is 1692. The same 1692 Lara traveled to before, in several weeks; An earthquake in Port Royal, Jamaica kills 3,000; John Arbuthnot publishes Of the Laws of Chance, *the first work on probability in English; the tractrix, often called a equitangential curve, is studied by Christin Huygens, whose name is attached to it; in the midst of a famine in Mexico City, the Viceroy's palace is torched but many key documents and paintings are saved by the royal geographer; Spanish colonists in what would become New Mexico, retake Santa Fe from the Pueblo after being kicked out twelve years earlier.*

"Anything you learned that I should know?" Lara asked. "Do you think I regressed since last we met?"

"You're from the Shadow," Pandora said. "Does your Time Patrol know that?"

"Yeah. Scout and I stopped by the Shadow's timeline on the way back last time. We saw them growing more of me. In the same place they grow the Legion."

Pandora blinked in surprise. "You went there? No one can get there."

"On the way back," Lara said. "A little side trip."

"Scout was with you?" Pandora didn't seem overly concerned with the dagger at her neck, although she'd just tried to behead Lara. "That's incredible. We've tried to break through . . ." She didn't finish the sentence.

Lara pulled the knife back. She picked up the Naga staff as she stood. "I'll be keeping this. Now, run away like you did last time when things got tough. The Time Patrol knows what I am. The big problem is *I'm* not sure I know what I am. But I know what I'm doing here. I'm going to save Unity Hale."

Some things change, some don't.

"Be sure you put your feet in the right place. Then stand firm."
Abraham Lincoln

WASHINGTON D.C.. 22 September 1862

eagle WASN'T THERE, and then he was there, but he'd sort of always been there. It was the best way to explain how he arrived, becoming part of his current time and place without fanfare or excitement among those around him. He was standing in an empty hallway, facing a door that was less than six inches from his nose.

He looked left and right, saw no one, then accepted the inevitable. He turned the knob and entered the room. A dour, frumpy woman in layers of petticoats and the other accouterments of a lady of moderate means in this time period, was seated in a chair in the small room. Eagle filled most of the rest of it, stopping just a few feet in front of her, blinking, trying to figure out where he was and who she was.

"You're a Negro!"

"Indeed," Eagle said and his cover story for this mission coalesced in an instant.

The woman adjusted quickly and bobbed her head in greeting. "Good day, sir." She had grey hair pulled up in a bun, two pins stuck through it.

"Good day," Eagle automatically responded. There were no windows in the room, which contained the chair, a small desk, the woman, and now Eagle.

The woman didn't get up and Eagle realized she was in a wheelchair.

"I assume you are the one I am expecting?" the woman said.

Eagle had no clue. "Yes."

"I'm the Keep." She waited to see if he knew what that meant.

"I'm in the White House?" Eagle asked.

"Yes." She frowned. "You came into the building. What an odd question."

"Sorry," Eagle said. "I'm a little confused."

"You know who I am?" the Keep asked.

"I know the job," Eagle said. "You keep the Book of Truths."

The woman smiled. "Ah! This is so exciting."

"You were expecting me?" Eagle asked.

"I didn't know who or what to expect," the Keep said.

It is 1862.; the USS Monitor *is launched; Peruvian slave traders land on Easter Island setting off a decade of devastation for the population; the Bureau of Revenue Service (AKA the IRS) is established; Les Miserables is published; the government of Vietnam cedes numerous territories to the French; Otto Von Bismarck becomes prime minister of Prussia; Richard Gatling patents a rapid fire gun and is promptly ignored; Anna Leonowens accepts an offer by the King of Siam to tutor his wives and children; William Lincoln, third son to the President and his wife, dies; the first petroleum export from the United States to England; the* USS Monitor *sinks off Cape Hatteras.*

The Keep pointed at a leather-bound book and Eagle could see that the hand was shaking from some sort of disorder. "There was an annotation from the very first Keep. She was appointed by Jefferson and served through five presidents, passing the book to her successor just before the end of President Madison's term. It's an odd note," she added. "Sally Hemings came to see her not long after Thomas Jefferson expired. She told the Keep a strange story of unique visitors that Thomas Jefferson experienced in 1776, and then on his death bed in 1826. Both concerned a Declaration of Emancipation. A man in 1776. A woman in 1826, who was foretold in detail by the visitor in 1776, which is quite unusual, you must admit."

"Interesting," Eagle said. There was a stool wedged in the corner. "May I sit?"

"Oh my, I'm so sorry. Certainly. I don't get visitors in here, thus my manners lack practice."

Eagle sat down. "Yes. One of my group met Jefferson in 1776 in Philadelphia. The Committee of Five had a Declaration of Emancipation prepared but it had to be shelved in order to get Independence passed. Another of my group was there on President Jefferson's last day."

"'Your group'?" the Keep asked.

"My people," Eagle said. "We've been here in North America for centuries since the first slaves were brought here in 1526 by the Spanish to South Carolina. We are much older than the United States. Doesn't it make sense we would have a secret core organized? And that we would be concerned and focused on Emancipation?"

"I never thought of that," the Keep said.

"It is all my people think of," Eagle said. "It is our lives. Why did you expect me today?"

"Because Sally Hemings told my predecessor that." The Keep retrieved the Book of Truths. She put it on the only clear part of a crowded desktop. Opened the cover, then carefully turned heavy pages made of parchment until she found the notation which was noted by a thin red ribbon book mark. "The entry was made in late 1826." She read the flowing script:

"*On the 22nd Day of September, the Equinox in the year of Our Lord, Eighteen Hundred and Sixty-Two, there will be a visitor. Much as President Jefferson had been foretold on the 4th of 1776, that there would be a visitor on the fiftieth anniversary of the Signing in 1826. This information was provided by Sally Hemings, an associate of President Jefferson during a brief visit to the Capitol.*"

"'Associate'?" Eagle repeated. "She was his slave and lover."

A tinge of red crept onto the Keep's face and she didn't meet Eagle's eye. "She had information." She continued reading. "*She spoke not only of the visitor who had been foretold, but a vision she had* *shortly afterward by what she claimed was an angel. Normally, such a statement would be considered frivolous but the specificity of the vision and the date and what was imparted is significant enough for me to note. Especially as it is consistent with what President Jefferson confirmed with his early entries about what happened on the 4th of July 1776 in the early morning hours in Philadelphia.”*

"That's it?" Eagle asked. "Just that someone is going to show up today?" An angel, which meant that a Valkyrie had paid Heming a visit.

"It *is* very strange that you've arrived today," the Keep noted. "It seems a confluence of events are merging."

"How so?" Eagle asked.

"Hemings not only predicted your arrival, she also brought something with her that she requested be kept secret until this particular day and the arrival of a visitor." The Keep opened a drawer and removed a leather bag. She pulled out a Jefferson Cipher.

"That was thrown into the fire at Monticello," Eagle said, even though he realized the inanity of the statement as the words came forth.

"One was according to the report," the Keep said. "But this was a twin, which Jefferson had hidden. Hemings knew where it was. She claimed he'd forgotten about it in his old age."

"Did this vision instruct Hemings to bring the cipher here?"

"Not just the cipher," the Keep responded. She opened another draw and withdraw a wooden tube. "She used it to uncover the original, signed, Declaration of Emancipation. It rests inside." She frowned. "But the other visitors that Hemings spoke of were not Negroes."

"They were sympathetic to our cause and could gain entry," Eagle explained. Before the Keep could respond, the air was rent by a horrendous scream from somewhere down the hall.

"Oh dear," the Keep said. She put the tube on her desk. She indicated the chair. "Please take me to her."

Eagle swung the door open and got behind the wheelchair. He pushed her into the hallway. "To who?"

"Mrs. Lincoln, of course," the Keep said. "Isn't that why you're here?"

Some things change, some don't.

"The Book of Mormon is the most correct of any book on this Earth, and the keystone of our religion, and a man would get nearer to God by abiding by its precepts, than any other book."
Joseph Smith. The Book of Mormon.

MANCHESTER, NEW YORK. 22 September 1823

Roland WASN'T THERE, and then he was there, but he'd sort of always been there. It was the best way to explain how he arrived, becoming part of his current time and place without fanfare or excitement among those around him except for the Chimera that tried to impale him with its barbed tail.

Roland was prepared, because Roland was always prepared. Fortunately for Roland, the Chimera seemed slightly out of sorts with his sudden appearance and Roland was able to dodge the strike from the beast's tail and take several steps back to assay his tactical situation.

The mythical, but very real, Chimera had the body of a lion, the head of a serpent and, as he'd just dodged, the tail of a scorpion.

"You're an ugly bastard," Roland said as he readied the Naga staff. He was pleased with this development as he'd faced Grendels and other beasts on missions, but never a Chimera. Scout and Lara had both encountered one and he'd felt left out. Which reminded him that Eagle had also battled one during the Black Tuesday mission. Roland figured it was his turn to answer the challenge.

He gave more ground, getting the sense of the enemy. He'd questioned the others about the beast to the point where they'd had to avoid him for a while, but how often does one come across a monster of legend?

Actually, dangerously often if one is in the Time Patrol.

A long tongue darted out of the snake head mouth and Roland tried to remember what it was about snakes and their tongues. Did they smell with them? Did it matter? The fangs were most definitely something to avoid, each about two inches long and dripping something that didn't seem like it would make him feel better.

Just kill it had been a Nada Yada when faced with a dangerous adversary, whether it was a rabbit possessed by a Firefly or anything threatening harm. Scout, or had it been Lara, or Eagle, had mentioned that the head moved in concert with the tail. Roland tracked it for a few moments and that was true. He figured it only had one brain and couldn't chew gum and walk at the same time. Nada had always had disdain for people packing two pistols —you could only aim one. The other was extra weight and often compensation for poor accuracy.

Roland had the range with the Naga staff. He hefted it with his right hand and approached. The snake head came at him and he jammed the tip of the spear directly into the creature's mouth, while watching for the tail. It came swinging around to impale him and he grabbed it with his left hand, barely stopping it before the barb struck his chest. Man and beast remained in balance for several seconds, both straining. Roland pushed his right arm, muscles bulging and the Naga spear penetrated deeper, through the roof of the mouth, into the Chimera's brain.

That, of course, didn't kill it. Gum and walking aside, it was a genetic monster designed to kill and the instinct went deeper than whatever passed for consciousness in its little brain. It did, however, perceptibly diminish the beast's strength.

Roland suddenly jerked the Naga back, out of the beast's mouth and whirled, still holding the scorpion tail. He swung the Naga blade down, severing the head. Roland then jerked the blade up and cut off the tail, tossing it aside as he dodged the squirming jaws which were death throe snapping on the ground.

Breathing hard, Roland moved back several paces while deciding which exercises he'd have to increase reps on in his workout so killing a Chimera wouldn't be so hard. The jaws slowly ceased their movement and the body stopped thrashing.

Roland brought the Naga up to do a few more skewerings of the body. After all, Nada has always howled in derision when they'd watched movies in the Ranch and someone had walked away from an enemy, not confirming they were dead, only to suffer revenge later from the supposedly vanquished opening. *Make sure it's dead, then make doubly sure*, had been a Nada Yada, which Roland thought quite reasonable.

However, as he closed in, the three pieces of the Chimera crumpled to dust.

Dead as a doornail. For a moment Roland wondered where that saying came from, then, even more puzzled, he wondered why he wondered. *Back on mission.*

The download confirmed he was on a currently un-named hill near Manchester, New York. In the future from now, it would be named Cumorah by Mormons and the surrounding land purchased as a monument to the spot where their religion began. But right now, it was just a wooded hill in the midst of farmland and Roland could smell manure in the breeze.

"Great," he muttered.

It is 1823. Work begins on the British Museum in London; the Presi-

dent introduces the Monroe Doctrine; the sport of rugby is invented;
Simon Bolivar becomes president of Peru; Tsar Alexander I draws up a
secret manifesto designating his second younger brother to rule after
him, rather than the traditional elder brother—this would have conse-
quences down the line during the Ides of March mission and Tsar
Nicholas; James Weddell's Antarctic Expedition reaches 74 degrees 15
minutes south, the farthest south anyone has ever gone, a record that
will stand for eighty years.

The west side of the hill was where Smith had found, *would find*, the plates inside of a stone sarcophagus. Roland looked up and oriented himself on the stars. Western side. Given the Chimera had been here, that doubly confirmed that the location was close by.

Roland wished he had some night vision goggles but no technology ahead of its time was allowed on a mission. It stood to reason that the Shadow would have the location under surveillance. The download informed Roland that Smith claimed to have been visited three times by the Angel Moroni the previous evening to let him know the plates would be here this morning.

Which Roland found weird, because wouldn't one angel/Valkyrie visit be enough? Or was the man a little slow on the angelic uptake?

The angel had also warned that Smith had to abide by certain commandments in order to be able to see the tablets. What those commandments were has been debated over the years but some were decided upon according to the download:

That Smith not use the tablets for monetary gain.

That he tell his father about the vision.

That he never show the plates to any 'unauthorized' person. Roland found this one awfully convenient.

That Smith wear black clothes. Roland glanced at his own outfit and realized a reason for it. Maybe Smith was looking for a black shirt before he came out here?

That Smith ride a black horse, which seemed really specific and why the heck was that important? Roland wondered.

That Smith give thanks to God.

The more Roland accessed the download, the more confused he got, so he decided to focus on the here and now which is what he usually did after accessing the download; after all it hadn't predicted the Chimera waiting here for him. The key piece of information was that this morning, just before dawn, Smith was supposed to find the plates for the first time; however, he didn't actually recover them until 1827.

Which also didn't make sense. This higher power seemed sort of a tease.

Roland figured he would wait until Smith showed up, took a gander, and left. Then Roland would gather them and either be brought back to the Possibility Palace or something else would occur. Whatever happened four years from now was not part of his mandate; unless of course he got sent back here again, like Lara had been sent back to Salem. He'd worry about that when that happened.

"Whatever," Roland muttered as he looked for a good spot to wait it out.

He didn't have to wait long as three Valkyries appeared out of a gate. Two of them carried a stone sarcophagus between them on poles.

Some things change, some don't.

"Tickling the dragon's tail."
Richard Feynman on criticality experiments with nuclear cores.

AREA 51. 22 September 1947

MOMS WASN'T THERE, and then she was there, but she'd sort of always been there. It was the best way to explain how she arrived, becoming part of her current time and place without fanfare or excitement among those around her. But not without notice as a bespectacled man turned from the blackboard he'd been writing on and ordered her: "Get me some coffee, hon."

He went back to his equations as Moms got oriented.

She was in a large cavern and the standing blackboard was one that rolled. There were several others scattered around, covered with calculations. There were large flat tables with schematics on them. Beyond the immediate work area, there were aircraft and rockets situated through the large hanger carved into the side of Groom Mountain, part of Area 51, which was under the overall control of Majestic-12.

The download identified each as Moms looked at them: V-1 and V-2 rockets. Several German Me 262 Schwalbe (Swallow) jet fighter-bombers. Moms paused the download because she knew the history of Area 51 from her time with the Nightstalkers. This was the skunkworks where the military and intelligence agencies were dissecting the aeronautics from the Third Reich in efforts to develop their own advanced airframes.

It is 1947. The United States begins the National Malaria Eradication Program which will wipe out malaria in four years; something crashes at Roswell, New Mexico, some say weather balloon, some say otherwise; Truman establishes the CIA; Thor Heyerdahl sails Kon Tiki across the Southern Pacific Ocean; Pakistan is carved out of India into a separate nation and the two nations will fight their first war within a few months; a moth caught in a relay of the Harvard Mark II computer causes it to malfunction leading to the first computer 'bug'; The United States Air Force is founded; Chuck Yeager breaks the speed of sound; the AK-47 is invented and will become the most popular assault rifle in history; the Marshall Plan to rebuild Europe is introduced; Elizabeth Short is murdered and would become known as the Black Dahlia.

And apparently women were supposed to get coffee and could be called 'Hon'.

Moms spotted the coffee pot. She poured a cup and brought it to the scientist. The download gave her a name: Dr. Kevin Brown.

"Here you are, sir," Moms said, holding out the cup.

Without looking, Brown fumbled for it, still focused on the board. Moms pushed it into his grasp. Once sure he had it, Moms stepped back, taking in her surrounding more carefully. She remembered this hanger and while the airframes were older, not much was different. There was a group of engineers crawling over a disassembled Me 262, marking the parts. There were several prototype American jet fighters such as the P-59 Airacomet and the Lockheed P-80 Shooting Star, but with advanced modifications from the designs developed near the end of World War II.

None of this was why she was here. Deeper underneath the mountain was where Odessa was working—the organization of former German and Japanese scientists gathered up by American intelligence agencies under the auspices of Operation Paperclip.

While those such as Werner Von Braun worked more openly, the ones here at Area 51 were the physicists, chemists, biologists and other specialties whose area of expertise were both cutting edge and controversial. Some of the men were responsible for horrendous atrocities, whether it be developing poison gasses that had been used on millions or developing biological agents and using them on test subjects, such as the Japanese from the infamous Unit 731.

Since Brown was enraptured by his work, Moms took the opportunity to go deeper into the hanger, to the entrance to the elevator that went down to the Odessa work area. Two heavily armed men with submachine guns stood guard at a steel door. They wore unmarked fatigues: no unit patches, no rank, no special awards. The way they held the weapons indicated they knew how to use them and the look in their eyes indicated combat veterans.

Moms pulled out the ID card she'd been issued and hoped the analysts had it correct.

One of the guards checked it, then nodded. Moms realized it made sense it appeared authentic since support had the actual records in their files to copy it from. It was her first cover, but she doubted it would go far for her presence below. For that, she had several sheets of paper folded inside a pocket in her business jacket.

As the guard handed her back the card, Moms looked behind her. The download informed her that Dr. Brown, still mesmerized by whatever theoretical problem he was working on, was going to be dead in less than four hours.

Neither guard opened the door for her. She tugged on the latch and pulled. As she did so, she realized those two men would most likely be part of the first Nightstalker team. Their data was in the download, but she stopped the influx, a technique she'd learned over the course of the missions. She didn't want to know whether they were going to die later today if she was going to be fighting alongside them. She paused as the door slowly shut behind her,

Some things change, some don't.

The door slammed shut.

Things all go past and they fade away.
After each December there comes another May.
German song, popular in 1940s

BERLIN. 22 September 1948

NEELEY WASN'T THERE, and then she was there, but she'd sort of always been there. It was the best way to explain how she arrived, becoming part of her current time and place without fanfare or excitement among those around her.

In fact, no one around her would have noticed much of anything as they were covered in coal dust and exhausted and numbingly shoveling away. She looked down at the shovel in her hands and the pile of coal in front of her. The air was full of a fine black mist and she experienced an immediate affinity for coal-miners and their relationship with black lung. But this coal wasn't in a mine. It was the back of a C-47 Dakota cargo plane.

Then she was noticed as the old woman next to Neeley shot her a dirty look and Neeley realized she needed to work. She retrieved a shovel full and carried it to the side cargo door where an open bed truck was waiting, engine running. She tossed the load inside. Three American soldiers were standing to the side of the truck, smoking and chatting, but they dropped the smokes and snapped to attention as an officer strode up, exuding no nonsense, a stopwatch in hand.

"You're behind!" he shouted.

For the first time Neeley noticed the peculiar and distantly familiar Berlin chill cutting through the threadbare coat she'd been supplied with. She wished support wasn't so particular at times. It wasn't winter yet, but it was coming and Berlin winters were dark and cold and the days were extremely short at this northern latitude.

"They gave us mostly a bunch of old ladies, General," a man with captain's bars complained.

"Where's the flight crew?" the General demanded.

Neeley scooped another load of coal from the cargo bay and dumped it in the truck, following the conversation.

"The snack bar, sir," the captain said. "I'm in command of the trucks."

"If you're leaning, you're loading," the General ordered. He pointed to the two enlisted men. "Grab shovels. This plane needs to be back in the air in fifteen minutes." To the captain. "Get the air crew back here now. And tell your other truck crews there's no standing around. Everyone works!"

The captain wasn't happy, but he scurried off. The two soldiers climbed up into the C-47. Neeley tossed another shovel load of coal and then noticed that the General was staring at her.

"You speak English?" He shouted at her. "You were listening, weren't you?"

Neeley nodded.

"*Frau, komm,*" he ordered.

Neeley felt a chill, remembering older, broken women in shattered buildings; women aged years past their time with a dead look in their eye that reflected the broken spirit inside of them. The ones who'd been in Berlin when the Soviets steamrolled into the city, losing as many men taking the city as the Americans lost in the entire war. Such was the fury of the Soviets toward Hitler's regime.

It is 1948. President Truman signs Executive Order 9981, desegregating the military; Mahatma Gandhi is assassinated in India; the House Un-American Activities Committee accuses Alger Hiss of spying for the Soviet Union; communists seize power in Czechoslovakia; the U.S. Congress ratifies the Marshall Plan, approving $17 billion in European aid; the Arab-Israeli War of 1948 follows the announcement of the independence of the state of Israel on May 14, 1948; the transistor is invented; the median family income in the United States is $3,200; the Soviet Union begins to jam the Voice of America radio broadcasts.

One of the enlisted men scowled at her as she handed him her shovel. She climbed out of the plane, onto the truck and then to the tarmac. The download gave her the officer's identity now that she could see him. General Bill Tunner, the mastermind behind molding the Berlin Airlift into the most efficient flying supply line since the Burma Hump, which he'd also commanded and where he'd learned what he was applying here.

Neeley recalled the accent she'd had from her time in Berlin. "Yes, General, I speak English. And you should not say those two words to a woman of Berlin."

Tunner didn't seem offended. "Why?"

"Those words were what Russians called to the women they were going to rape."

Some things change; some don't.

"You speak excellent English," Tunner said.

"Thank you."

"Under that coal dust you're a good-looking woman," Tunner said.

Neeley put her hands on her hips. She looked down slightly on the shorter general.

Tunner held up a hand in apology. "I don't mean it in the *Frau, komm* way or anything like that. What I want is to get these damn planes off the ground fast. Quicker than we're doing. The pilots have a tough track coming in. They do need a cup of hot coffee and something to wolf down before they make the turn around and while the plane is unloaded. But wandering off to the snack bar in the terminal causes some of them to be late. That bunches up the line and accordions the slow down.

"I don't want the crews leaving the damn plane. I want to bring the snack bar to them. And I want good looking women serving them coffee and snacks. Because it would be good for morale, and when morale is better, this whole damn thing works more efficiently and we've got a ways to go to improve in order to make sure your people don't freeze to death this winter." He smacked the side of the truck as he finished.

It was a heck of a speech and Neeley saw why Tunner was good at what he did. He cut to the heart of the matter. He was good with numbers and schedules, but most importantly, he knew it was motivation that drove all those statistics.

Coal was the most important factor because it was heat, it was power, it was cooking. Before Tunner arrived, the commander before him had tried air dropping sacks of it into the remains of the stadium that had hosted the 1936 Olympics. That had quickly proved ineffective as the bags exploded on impact leaving unusable fragments and coal-laden air.

"It is a good idea, General," Neeley said.

"Glad you approve," Tunner said, but his tone indicated he appreciated her immediate agreement rather than sarcasm. "I'm going to give you a written order with authorization."

The massive Tempelhof Terminal was one of the largest buildings in the world at this time, a huge semi-circle over a kilometer long. From the air, the terminal and the flanking hangers, had been designed to look like an eagle in flight. Although slated by Hitler to be destroyed during the last days of the war, the German commander had opted to suicide rather than blow the airport up.

"You get the best looking of your fellow female workers, pull them from loading, and set up a mobile snack bar out here. Service ten planes at a time. Anyone gives you a hard time, you show them the order. Got it?"

He didn't wait for an answer. Tunner immediately began doing what he said; he opened a leather binder and was rapidly writing on a piece of paper with his letterhead on it. He signed it, handed the paper to Neeley, and snapped the binder shut.

"Get to work."

AREA 51

"Aren't we taking the long way around?" Ivar asked Colonel Orlando as he drove them away from the long runway that stretched along the desert floor. The plane which had flown Angus and Ivar here from New York at hypersonic speed had never shut down and it was already accelerating down the runway to take off.

Instead of heading toward the open hanger doors set in the side of Groom Mountain, Orlando was driving into the desert along a route Ivar vaguely recalled from his days in the Nightstalkers, which hadn't been that many, before they became the Time Patrol.

"I got reasons," Orlando said and that satisfied Angus, but not Ivar who always had to know why.

Angus had greeted the old Colonel with a handshake, but not a word as he threw their gear into the back of the aging Jeep. Ivar had bowed to inevitable and taken the rickety seat in the rear, next to the two rucksacks they had brought with them. Orlando wore rumpled fatigues with the silver oak leaf of a light colonel on his collar, but that was the military around here, because the military needed things like that to figure out where in the pecking order someone was and Orlando was too old and too irritable to have to pull out his ID card, which actually proved he held the rank equivalent of a two star general in GS—government service. He only pulled that card, which was as much a lie as the silver oak leaf, when he needed to access secure places. To a civilian it might make more sense to wear two stars, but Orlando had actually served in the Army long enough to know that a two-star general meandering around drew way too much attention. A light colonel was in a middling ground of enough rank to wander around and low enough to draw little notice.

It was complicated, but Area 51 is a complicated place. There were military, spooks, civilian contractors and all sorts working out of it on an array of projects. This had been so ever since it was founded during World War II. It is deliberately in the middle of nowhere on the way to nowhere. West of it is the Nevada Test Site where the government has officially exploded 739 nuclear warheads and reasonable people would think twice and then decide not to cross. The official count was a smidge low, given the Nightstalker's experiences. North was the Nellis Air Force Range, full of unexploded ordnance since the government gave contracts to people who lobbied the best, not necessarily built the best bomb. Once more, a reasonable person would decide against going overland.

"Are we going to the Ranch?" Ivar finally asked as Orlando turned onto a dirt road that was definitely familiar.

In reply, Orlando reached into a deep pocket and produced a flask. He expertly unscrewed the top, took a draft, and passed it to Angus.

"On the clock, friend," Angus said, declining.

Orlando held it toward Ivar.

"No, thanks," Ivar said.

Orlando shrugged. "Might want a little fortification given this clusterfuck."

"What clusterfuck?" Ivar asked.

Ivar involuntarily ducked as a Snake flew by overhead so low, they could smell and feel the jet fuel exhaust in their face. The twin-jet-engined tilt wing aircraft, several generations more advanced than the Osprey deployed in the military, banked hard and swung around again, taking a look-see of the occupants of the Jeep. The chain gun under the cockpit tracked them as it went by, then it headed for the Barn, its hangar, which was part of the Ranch, where the Nightstalkers were home-based.

The Jeep crested a ridgeline and a two-lane highway stretched perpindicular across their route. It was a lonely road and even though they could see to the horizon left and right, there were no vehicles on it. Going downhill, the Jeep picked up speed. The road was Nevada Route 375, aka Extraterrestrial Highway. Orlando drove directly across it.

All the alien/UFO enthusiasts who came out this far always looked to the west of Route 375, because that's where Area 51 is. It didn't occur to them something could be east, which was why the Nightstalkers had moved from Area 51 to the Ranch many years ago. At least that had been what Ivar had been briefed and was in the book Angus had consumed so thoroughly. The Ranch was on private land, which made it more secure than federal Area 51 because Nevada's Stand Your Ground Law, dating back to the Wild West of 1871, allowed Ranch security to gun down anyone who crossed its boundaries.

Ivar recognized the same spray-painted plywood No Trespass: We Will Shoot Your Ass sign with skull and crossbones next to the dirt road. A bit more faded. Ahead on the right was what appeared to be an abandoned gas station. Orlando threw the clutch in neutral and began rolling to a stop, seconds before two men appeared out of spider holes on either side of the road, weapons at the ready. Ivar and Angus had red dots on their chest.

"Must be hot in those holes," Angus commented as the Jeep halted. He was looking back and Ivar followed his gaze. A third man dressed in black combat gear was coming up from behind. He walked around to Orlando and passed a handheld scanner over Orlando's face, making sure to get the eyes.

"Look at me," he ordered and both Ivar and Angus complied. He scanned their eyes. Without a word he turned and walked away. The two other guards had already disappeared back in their holes.

Orlando ground the stick shift into gear and they pulled up to the deserted gas station. A decrepit, rusting soda machine was to the left of the door.

"Gas prices give one a feel for the time this place might have been open," Angus said, pointed to faded numbers on a sign. "Seventies?"

Orlando shrugged. "I don't think there ever was a gas station here. Support built it. You'll see."

"That I will." Angus got out of the Jeep and tossed one of the rucksacks to Ivar, who dropped it.

"You got explosives in there, lad," Angus said.

"What?" Ivar paused in picking it up.

Angus laughed. "Don't you be worrying." He tapped his breast pocket. "I'm carrying the fuses close to me heart."

Orlando turned off the engine and got out, slapping dust and sand out of his fatigues. Ivar carefully slung the rucksack over his shoulder and headed for the soda machine, which appeared nonfunctional. The peeling labels gave a choice once upon a time of Dr. Pepper, Pepsi, Orange or Grape. Another indicator of age was the price: 25c.

"Don't do grape," Orlando warned just as Ivar reached for that button. "They do change things up, you know."

Ivar stepped back. "Maybe you should lead."

"It's a thought," Orlando said. He hit Dr. Pepper and with a hiss of hydraulics, the soda machine slid to the side and a stairway beckoned, cool air blasting out.

"We have eight seconds," Orlando warned. Ivar scurried in, followed by Angus at a leisurely pace, then Orlando.

"Welcome to the Ranch," a man standing at the bottom of the stairs greeted them. Of course, since he was a Nightstalker, he had a gun aimed at them.

THE MISSIONS PHASE II

NEW YORK CITY, 22 September 1776

"I was bringing the prisoner food and drink as General Howe ordered," Scout protested. She was assessing the tactical situation and felt pretty confident she could take Rogers even though he had the pistol, but that would also change history and screw up the mission. Plus, it would piss off all the present day Rangers like Eagle and Moms.

Time travel was a pain in the ass.

"You were doing more than that," Major Rogers said.

The download was pouring material about Rogers into her brain and she schizoided for the moment, trying to keep her wits in the present and seeking something usable from the data.

Rogers had initially gained notoriety for forming his Ranger company during the French and Indian War. He was celebrated in Scout's present for that company's daring raids behind enemy lines and also for Rogers Rules of Rangering which seemed like Nada's Yadas: common sense one liners that were smart soldiering.

But the details indicated Rogers was anything but an upstanding soldier. He'd been in prison several times for debt and even brought up on charges of treason to the King as the royal governor of a distant outpost at Mackinac in Michigan.

"Sounded to my ears as if you desired to help the prisoner escape," Rogers said.

"I was enquiring after his welfare and connection with the Lord, the friend to all of us," Scout argued. "He asked for a Bible but none was provided. Why not?"

Rogers' face grew even redder. "How dare you speak to me like that." He stepped forward, within easy knife range, and slapped Scout hard on the cheek. She went with the blow, stumbling a bit and resisted gutting the man.

"A gentleman does not strike a lady!" Nathan Hale was on his feet, the letter falling to the ground.

"A gentleman isn't a skulking spy," Rogers countered as he stepped back, covering both of them with his pistol. "You said you were his friend," he said to Scout. "That you were going to help him escape. I heard it."

"I said no such thing," Scout argued, putting as much earnestness in her voice as possible. "I asked if anyone had contacted him about the Bible."

"And why would you be asking him that?" Rogers demanded.

"She did exactly what you trapped me with yesterday," Hale said to Rogers. "Pretending to be a patriot when you are nothing of the sort. Why accuse her of what you are guilty of?"

Rogers scoffed at that. "You're a piss poor example of a spy and deserve to hang. Using an alias yet carrying your diploma from Yale with your actual name on it."

Hale had no response to that, which Scout's download confirmed had been the case. Hale would have failed Tradecraft 101 at Fort Bragg.

"I was following General Howe's orders," Scout said with complete conviction.

"I heard what the General told you to do," Rogers said, but his voice was a bit less certain. He took a quick look over his shoulder as the greenhouse door squeaked open and Captain Montressor entered. The British officer drew his pistol upon seeing the confrontation.

"What is going on?" Montressor demanded.

"This wench is conspiring with the prisoner," Rogers said.

"To do what?" Montressor asked.

"To escape."

"I was doing no such thing!" Scout protested. "The prisoner asked for a clergyman and a Bible. Should not a condemned man have those?"

Montressor raised an eyebrow as he tucked the pistol back into his belt. "He looks well on his way to freedom, eh, Rogers? And that young waif seems the dangerous sort, doesn't she?"

"That's Major Rogers to you, Captain."

Montressor laughed. "I know all about you, Rogers. You're no loyalist. You go to the highest bidder. You offered your services to the rebels but they didn't trust you. I don't trust you and the General doesn't either. Get out of here and leave this man to his last hours in peace." He checked a pocket-watch. "He only has two left. Today will be difficult enough without your interference, Rogers."

SALEM, MASSACHUSETTS. 22 September 1692

"Perhaps you're going to kill Unity," Pandora argued.

"You're not as bright as you think you are," Lara said as she continued toward Salem, Naga staff in hand. "If I was gonna do that, I'd have done it on my last mission, later this year." She laughed. "That's not something you can say every day. Besides. No Unity. No Scout. And Scout is my friend. It's my mission."

Lara reached the dark village square. A crude gallows dominated the area. A beam supported by wooden tripods on either end. The same as the one she'd seen on her last visit. Except for the eight nooses drooping from the beam.

Lara stood still, scanning the village. It was quiet, windows shuttered. The download gave her a best guess where the condemned were, but that wasn't her mission. History had written that eight would be hung at dawn and there was nothing she could do about that. Which, of course, wasn't true. There was a lot she could do if she wanted to violate the first rule of the Time Patrol and change history.

Where was Unity? The download was no help in that.

Lara closed her eyes and focused her mind.

She heard Pandora, standing nearby, say something, but the 'goddess' was background noise, of no significance at the moment. Lara was 'looking' for Unity Hale, recalling the young girl's aura during the last mission. There was no sense of her in the village, but Pandora's presence was distracting. Lara opened her eyes.

"Why are you here?" Lara demanded of Pandora. "You were around last time, but bugged out as soon as things got a little difficult. From what Scout told me, I figured you'd be tougher."

"You handled it," Pandora said. "After all, you're back."

"You knew I'd be here," Lara said. *Where was Unity?*

"She's not in town," Pandora said.

"I know that," Lara replied. "I wasn't asking you because my lips didn't move."

"But you were asking loudly in your head," Pandora said. "Might want to get some control over that."

"Screw you." Lara faced her. "You knew I'd be back. There was never any question when this came up as a mission that it would be mine. You're here for me."

"No," Pandora said. She pointed with her Naga staff to Lara's left rear. "I'm here for him."

Standing in the moonlight dappled shadows at the edge of Salem was Lukas. A Lukas.

"Hello, sister," he said.

WASHINGTON D.C.. 22 September 1862

Eagle pushed the Keep down the hall toward the sound of Mary Todd Lincoln. Eagle was trying to factor in the presence of the original Declaration of Emancipation to today's events. What difference would it make? What was the Shadow trying to set up? There was no record of it being found in the download. Eagle was feeling the presence of Dane's vagaries of the variables.

The scream descended to wretched sobs that were more distressing in their own way. Eagle didn't need directions to find the correct room; he just had to head toward the sound. The layout of the current White House was in the download and he'd accessed it before leaving the room and now had it memorized. He pushed the chair up to the door and the Keep leaned forward, turned the knob.

"My dear, my dear," the Keep called out and Eagle pushed her in, toward the distraught woman splayed over a couch near a cold fireplace.

Eagle recognized Mary Todd Lincoln and knew most of her history, which was often glossed over with an image much like what he was seeing now which saw her as a drain on Lincoln. The reality was that there was no doubt without her support, her husband would not have been able to achieve much of his greatness.

Historians suspect, in retrospect, that she had bipolar disorder, an affliction that wasn't understood in this day and age. She was in the midst of one of her episodes and Eagle positioned the Keep next to the couch.

The Keep placed a comforting hand on Mrs. Lincoln's shoulder and spoke in a soothing tone: "It will pass. It will pass."

Mrs. Lincoln was shaking her head. "No. It will not pass. It will never pass. I see their ghosts. Eddie and Willie. They want to talk to me but I cannot hear! Their mouths are moving but no words come forth."

She was referring to her two deceased sons: Edward Lincoln had died at the age of four in 1850 from tuberculosis and Willie was a fresh, raw scar on her psyche, passing earlier this year in February of typhoid fever. She'd taken to bed for three weeks and would never truly recover. The pathos of the future washed over Eagle, then he pushed it aside.

Mrs. Lincoln looked at the Keep. "And the worst part? They cannot hear me, either. I just know it. They cannot take comfort from my voice and from my words. They are lost in the void."

"They have moved on to a better place," the Keep said, "not the void."

Mrs. Lincoln abruptly swung her feet off the couch and sat up. She stared the Keep in the eyes. "You speak words to me for comfort, and I feel your earnestness behind them. I do appreciate your assistance. But tell me. If there is a God, why is he so cruel? Why does he allow so much death? My husband anguishes over the rolls of the casualties from Antietam. Over two thousand. Think of the mothers who are receiving letters telling them their boy no longer breathes; no longer feels the sun? That he died violently. Did he suffer? Did he linger? Did he experience the surgeon's blade removing a limb to die anyway? Was he shot in the stomach and died that agonizing path? Those are the questions that will cascade through their minds. How will *they* receive comfort?" Her voice rose as she spoke.

The Keep gave no response.

Eagle knew Antietam, even to his time, was the bloodiest day of combat in United States history. An epic confrontation that, ultimately, yielded no conclusive result for either side, although it did cause Robert E. Lee to retreat from Maryland across the Potomac back to Virginia.

"Will you speak words of comfort to all those mothers?" Mrs. Lincoln demanded.

"I wish I could," the Keep said. "But I am here for you. I feel your pain."

"What's the point?" Mrs. Lincoln demanded. "Is it worth all the pain for so many? Is it worth all the death?"

Eagle had stepped back, analyzing, trying to understand why he was here with the Keep. Why would the Shadow want the original Declaration of Emancipation passed by the same Congress that had ratified the Declaration of Independence to show up today, of all days? It could confuse things, certainly. But would it matter? Would it *change* anything?

The Keep leaned close to Mrs. Lincoln, lowering her voice, maintaining the comforting tone. She was murmuring something and it seemed to be working. The President's wife was calming down.

Eagle's musings were interrupted when the President came through a door on the far side of the room. His tall, thin figure filled the frame. Indeed, he had to duck slightly to enter. He paused, looking over each of the three: his wife, the Keep, and Eagle.

When the President's gaze touched him, Eagle felt that same aura he'd experienced with George Washington. There were rare men who had a presence that transcended and Abraham Lincoln was one. Lincoln's eyes narrowed briefly in his craggy, long face and he kept his eyes on Eagle for a few seconds, before he went to his wife and knelt next to her, nodding appreciatively at the Keep.

"Does your head hurt?" he asked his wife.

She indicated negatively. "No. I have had visions again."

Lincoln tried a smile. "Good ones, I pray?"

"Strange ones."

The relationship between the President and his wife was one that not only perplexed historians, it had confused contemporaries. Even Abraham, just a week after his marriage to her, had written in a letter to an acquaintance that the union was '*a matter of profound wonder*' to him. He'd even called off the wedding once. But historians tended to write about the woman Eagle was seeing here and now, not the younger, alluring version. The one that had drawn Stephen Douglas' ardor before she'd chosen his political rival. As Lincoln had an aura, so had Mary Todd. And while she had a dark side, so did Lincoln. He was often gloomy and sad, weighed down not just by the presidency, but by life itself, as the uncommonly brilliant often are. They were a curious combination that had produced a partnership that would somehow steer the United States through its greatest threat since its formation but end in tragedy for one and extended misery for the other.

Lincoln went from kneeling to sitting next to his wife. He did not put a supporting arm around her. In fact, there was a space between them that was palpable. "How strange?"

"Angels," Mary Todd said.

Eagle stiffened.

"At least they not were demons." Lincoln's jibe fell flat.

"They had a message," Mary Todd said.

Eagle waited for it.

"They spoke?" Lincoln asked.

Mary Todd pointed at her head. "I heard them. They had no mouths but their words were in the air. And they *were* real. Two them. All in white. But they had no wings, which was strange, although they hovered above me. Red eyes. No mouth, so, of course, they could not speak out loud. I see that now." The words were coming faster. "But I heard the message. You cannot do it. It will be your death. They predicted it."

Lincoln didn't seem bothered by the prediction. "We will all die, sooner or later."

"They predicted it sooner," Mary Todd said. "Within the year. Unless you refrain."

"From?" Lincoln asked. "What are you speaking of, my wife?"

"The Proclamation," Mary Todd said. "You cannot announce it. The Proclamation will be your doom." And then she threw herself into his chest, almost knocking him off the couch.

MANCHESTER, NEW YORK. 22 September 1823

Roland readied the Naga Staff. The Valkyries would have to wonder where their Chimera was. Or did they even care? It seemed the Shadow left some of their creatures behind, which helped give rise to their legends; it wasn't like anyone was going to be able to show an actual corpse since they always disappeared into dust.

Roland trailed the Valkyries through the woods for a quarter mile. They paused in a clearing and the two lowered the chest to the ground.

Roland hid himself behind the wide trunk of a large tree.

The three Valkyries backed up ten feet. Two of them went farther into the trees, out of sight. One remained, hovering a foot above the ground. Roland had to admit he'd be impressed seeing them if he didn't know what they were. For an ordinary person, they did seem otherworldly.

Which, obviously, Joseph Smith did because as he rode his black horse into the clearing, he fell off the horse upon seeing the Valkyrie, rather than dismount. He lay on the ground, apparently unconscious.

"Seriously?" Roland muttered to himself.

The horse remained in place, as bored as Roland was getting. Smith finally stirred, getting to his knees and raising his hands in supplication.

"I am here as commanded!" he cried out.

Roland was startled as a voice echoed inside his head and he realized he was hearing what the Valkyries was 'saying' to Smith.

"*I am the Angel Moroni.*"

Smith prostrated himself on the ground.

"*Rise up, Joseph Smith. You are the one I have chosen to bear my message. I am the last prophet of the chosen people whom God led forth from Jerusalem six hundred years before the birth of the one called Jesus, the eldest of God's children.*

"*Our people were led here, to this great land, long before any others by the prophet Lehi. Then the greatest prophet, Jesus, came and taught the Gospel directly to them, because they are chosen. In this case are gold plates that tell of this and more. They lay out the path you, our newest prophet, must take. It also contains the Urim and Thummim, stones which you will use to decipher the engravings.*

"*You will gaze upon the gold plates today, but you will not read them. Not yet. You must come back a year from now to receive further prophecies. And then four years from now you will bring them forth from this place. By then, we will know that your faith is true and you will be able to use the Thummim and Urim to translate them into a language your followers will understand.*"

The voice went on with more stuff about prophets and rules and all the other stuff that was part and parcel of the basis of any burgeoning religion.

Roland felt a chill, unnatural breeze and he spun about, leveling the Naga and swinging hard. The blade went through the person behind him with no resistance because she was there, but she wasn't there.

"That wasn't very polite," the old woman scolded. She raised her hand and the voice in Roland's head stopped mid-sentence. He looked over his shoulder and Joseph Smith was frozen in place. Even the leaves on the trees were still.

The old woman wore a white robe, a rod held in one hand across her body, the length of it in the crook of the other arm. It seemed Roland was getting to make up all his teammates had experienced. This was a Fate. The woman matched the description of Lachesis, the middle of the three. She was the disposer of lots; the one who determined how long the thread of life that Clotho, the first of the Fates initiated, would last. The rod was to measure life. She ruled not only the length of life, but also a person's destiny. The third Fate, Atropos, was the one who cut the thread and brought about the true death.

"You snuck up on me," Roland said. The Valkyrie was also frozen and he considered whether he should kill it and the other two hidden in the trees since they came from the Shadow.

"No, you may not," Lachesis.

"Get out of my head," Roland said.

"As you wish," she agreed. "Killing minions is not what I am here for." She looked him over. "Excellent. A strapping young man. Perfect for what is needed." She paused and sniffed. "There was a beast here?"

"A Chimera," Roland said. "I killed it."

"Bravo for you," Lachesis said. "Those beasts are genetic abominations. They violate the natural order of life." She strode forward. "Come along."

Roland followed Lachesis to the stone box, glancing at the Valkyrie to make sure it was frozen.

"Remove the lid," Lachesis ordered.

Roland pulled it off, grunting with the effort as it weighed at least a hundred pounds. The interior was packed with gold plates, each less than a sixteenth of an inch thick and stacked vertically on their sides. Twenty of them.

Lachesis touched each one briefly, going from left to right. "Curious," she muttered. She pointed with her rod, indicating the clearing. "Please lay them out so I might see them."

"All of them?" Roland asked.

Lachesis put the haft of the rod on the ground and the other hand on her hip. "Do you want me to help? An old woman? Is it too hard for you?"

"I'm here on a mission," Roland said.

"Do you think I'm here to exchange banter with you, young man? Your mission is my mission. Now. Get the plates."

Roland begrudgingly removed one of the plates. It was three feet long by two wide and solid, despite being so thin. He placed it down, the hieroglyphics facing up in the moon and starlight. Then the next. Lachesis walked over and stared down at the first as he worked. He was barely able to keep ahead of her, so he started grabbing four at a time. He was sweating in the chill September night by the time he had all twenty spread out and Lachesis was only three behind him.

"Yes," Lachesis said as she stood next to him at the base of the last one. "As expected and not good at all."

Roland couldn't make any sense of the markings on the tablet but it reminded him of what the people in the Pit used for writing. "What?"

"Some of these do not belong here," Lachesis said. "Some of what is on them does not belong. The Shadow is sowing confusion."

"Okay," Roland said, for lack of any other response. He waited but Lachesis wasn't forthcoming with anything further. "I think I can break them with my Naga staff," he offered.

Lachesis glanced at him, then chuckled and shook her head. "It would make sense a man such as you, a warrior, would go to destruction as the first option. There are better ways to deal with misdirection. Besides, these do serve an important function."

"Okay," Roland said. He waited a few beats, then asked. "Such as?"

"We take the tablets where they're supposed to go and put them in the correct order." She pointed with the rod. "We also remove the knowledge that shouldn't be on them. Pick up that one, that one, and that one. Put the rest back where they were."

Roland replaced seventeen tablets, skipping the three she'd designated.

Lachesis nodded. "Good. We'll start at the end and work our way to the beginning."

As Roland picked up the three, a Gate snapped open behind Lachesis. "Hurry now. The future is waiting."

AREA 51. 22 September 1947

The elevator crept downward at an excruciatingly slow pace, much slower than Moms remembered, but it had been upgraded by the time she joined the Nightstalkers, years from now. She absently started humming the *The Girl From Ipanema*, realized she was doing it and stopped. It shuddered to a halt and she pulled the doors open, to be met by two more guards.

"ID," one of them ordered, while the other kept a good field of fire on her.

She produced the identification card. The guard scanned it. "Never seen you down here before. This doesn't give clearance to enter."

"I work with Professor Brown."

"Brown isn't part of this team," the guard said. "Go back up."

Moms pulled out the paperwork Edith had provided for just this situation. "I am authorized to coordinate with Odessa."

The guard took it and carefully read. He looked up at her a couple of times, as if mystified that the person referenced in the documents was the same as the one standing in front of her.

"Cover her," he ordered his partner, which was redundant since he'd been doing that since the doors opened. He took the papers over to the black rotary phone. Dialed one number. Spoke in a low voice that Moms couldn't make out. He listened, then walked off with the papers toward a door in a wall full of them along the right side of the cavern.

She used the time to check out the work area. Years later the control room for the Can would be put far below this area, but for now it was full of equipment. There were several massive first-generation computers, cousins to the ENIAC that Moms had helped save the previous year in Philadelphia. She didn't spot any of the six women who'd kept that computer running in Philadelphia and the Shadow had tried to destroy. In fact, there weren't any women down here at all, which explained the guard's reaction; beyond that of scrupulously doing his job.

Were the computers the target?

There was a screen directly ahead, blocking her view of the center of the open area.

The true classified work of Odessa was here. Top end jet and rocket engines were being built. There was a large cylinder at the far end: a wind tunnel where various wing and rocket shapes were tested.

Today the Rift would open in here. Fireflies would come through, taking over inanimate objects. It would take all the guard personnel at Area 51 to figure out what was going on and stop them; most would die in the process. The survivors would become the Nightstalkers.

Did the Shadow want the Fireflies to break containment? Moms remembered how she'd and Nada had lectured the new members of the team about the three C's: Containment, Concealment and Control. She considered the possibilities of a containment breach. Despite closing over two dozen Rifts and encountering numerous Fireflies and destroying them, they were still no closer to understanding exactly what a Firefly was.

Fireflies came through as small golden sparkles, hence the name, that went into objects, whether animate or inanimate and took them over. They did not go into humans, though, for some unknown reason. They could control and turn whatever they took over into something deadly though, from a pool of water to a desert cactus, or a rabbit or a backhoe.

Moms, and the other Nightstalkers, had little empathy with careless scientific dabbling and she was looking at perhaps the penultimate of that. Most of the scientists in here, wearing their white coats as if they were innocent, were German or Japanese. The 'best and brightest' that could be spirited out of the burnt-out ruins of their home countries by the Office of Strategic Services during the waning months of World War II. This despite an explicit, public order by the President forbidding it. Secretly, Majestic-12 had gotten the OSS to initiate Operation Paperclip, an innocuous sounding code name for the project. After all, the Russians couldn't be allowed to catch up to American scientific expertise using Nazis and Japanese. The Americans would use them to learn from their wartime experiments that had been unrestrained from ethical considerations.

The ends justified the means.

The ones here, were the physicists and as far as Moms knew, and the download supplied, they hadn't conducted any such terrible things as the biologists and chemists with their poison gas. However, if either the Japanese or Germans had managed to crack the secret of the atom first, there is no doubt they would have used the bomb. Before the Americans did, that is. For the victors it had been a tool of war, not a war crime.

Moms shook off ethical musings as the guard came back with her papers. He handed them to her. "Sit there." He indicated a wood chair. She assumed whoever was in that office was making some phone calls.

Moms complied. Eventually, the door opened and an officer came out. Moms recognized the man striding toward her. Colonel Thorn. He had a scar cutting across his face from his left eye, across his nose, down to his right chin. A unique wound and she wondered what made it and blocked the download from filling that in, because it wasn't important right now. Even here, deep underground, he wore aviator glasses.

He looked at Moms, but not in the way men looked at women, but as a covert operative evaluating a peer. "Your papers are in order. What are you doing down here?"

Moms remembered Thorn. From the future. Coming back through the last Rift with the members of Odessa. "I'm to observe."

Thorn pursed his lips. "I report to Majestic-12 also. I'll be filing a complete report."

"They want a scientist's observations," Moms said.

A twitch of a smile. "You're a scientist?"

"That's what my paperwork says, correct?"

"Yeah," Thorn agreed in a way that indicated he didn't believe her, but understood the need for compartmentalization. "That's what the paper says." He checked his watch. "They're starting in forty-six minutes." He nodded at the guards. "She's cleared." Thorn walked away.

Moms stepped past the guards and could see around the screen. Fifty feet away, in the center of the cavern, spotted a large arch, twenty feet high, made of bright, shiny metal. A number of the scientists were gathered around it, checking wires that ran to various points along it. Most went to the computers, but others were power supplies.

The arch reminded her of when a Rift had been opened underneath the Gateway Arch in St. Louis. That had been bad because a former team-member, Burns, had come through and caused havoc. Which further reminded her that the man in charge of the scientists here was Colonel Johan Schmidt, who was, is, would be, that former team-member's grandfather

Moms was having a hard time keeping track of it all. Since Schmidt went through the Rift that would open soon, that meant his daughter was already born and would eventually give birth to

Burns, who'd been wounded badly during the clusterfuck in the desert outside of Tucson when the Nightstalkers shut down a Rift. Burns had then come back through the St. Louis Rift and caused considerable damage.

There was a buzz of excitement as two men rolled a cart to a position directly underneath the arch. On it was a dull grey metal sphere, 3.5 inches in diameter surrounded by a ring that was designed to keep the neutron flux from jetting when the dragon's tail was tickled:

The Demon Core.

BERLIN. 22 September 1948

Neeley had General Tunner's letter in hand and had already gotten the names of a half-dozen women to be promoted out of the coal shoveling brigade and into the snack bar beauty pageant. She didn't find the task sexist, because Tunner's realism and pragmatism, balanced with the necessity of the airlift, far superseded such concerns.

However, as she continued along the flight line, she was mentally scanning the download. The mobile snack bar would be a big hit with the pilots and help increase the efficiency of the airlift, cutting down on delays and improving morale among the exhausted and stressed pilots. Even with that, the download informed her that seventeen American and eight British aircraft would crash during the operation and there would be over a hundred fatalities. Nevertheless, Neeley didn't believe for a moment this was her mission. The Shadow wasn't going to sabotage hot coffee and snacks.

Neeley paused at the next truck, checking the workers: mainly old men, boys, and women of all ages. Men of military age were either dead or those who'd become POWs had been taken by the Russians into the far east to the gulag. No one expected them to come back. Over three million in total had been taken prisoner by the Russian. Over a million of those died before the end of the war. Another four hundred thousand would be dead by 1950, by which most would have been repatriated. Some, however, would still be held as late as 1956.

This was a waste of her time and she felt the clock ticking on this bubble of time.

She took a break and went inside the terminal. She checked the download and headed for an access point to the roof to get a better perspective. The Airlift was still in its early stages although it began on the 26th of June after the Soviet Union blocked all road, water and rail access to the former German capitol on the 24th. The Russian intent was to force the Allies to abandon the western part of the city. Since the city only had enough food for 36 days and coal for 45, the Soviets had thought it wouldn't take long before the Allies withdrew.

The air corridors into the city that had been negotiated at the end of the war were a different matter than road, rail or water. The only way to blockade those was to shoot the planes down and that would be an act of war. But pragmatic Soviet military planners didn't see how so many people could be resupplied via air. They also didn't believe the Allies would go to war over the fate of their former enemies, the Germans. On top of that, the United States and Britain had greatly dismantled their militaries after the peace. In Berlin itself, the Americans had only nine thousand troops in two undermanned regiments. Surrounding the city were over a million and a half Russian troops. The post-war Americans relied on their sole possession of the atomic bomb as a deterrence but they certainly wouldn't use it over Berlin. Not only that, but how could they? Where would they drop it to help the situation?

It seemed a win-win. The Soviets celebrated once they had the blockade established, believing a victory would soon be theirs.

However, there was more at stake than just a segment of the

former German capitol. The American general in charge of West Berlin cabled President Truman: *"There is no practicability in maintaining our position in Berlin and it must not be evaluated on that basis... We are convinced that our remaining in Berlin is essential to our prestige in Germany and in Europe. Whether for good or bad, it has become a symbol of the American intent."*

There were those among the Allied High Command, particularly General Curtis LeMay who pushed for an aggressive, belligerent response. Neeley didn't need the download to know about LeMay. From this time forward he was always pushing for military action against the Soviets until he died. He'd wanted to use his fledgling Air Force to cover an armored ground column advancing with supplies to Berlin, despites the logistics of it succeeding being slim to none and having a good chance of instigating World War III.

Neeley reached the roof and walked to the side facing the airfield. Planes were taxiing into position, forming a line to take off, in between the flights coming in. Landing aircraft had to fly over an apartment building at the edge of the airstrip and then drop quickly in order to touch down. She watched one swoop down on the steep descent. Just before it reached the edge of the airfield, dozens of small white specks blossomed in the wake of the aircraft.

Neeley smiled.

The Candy Bombers. A large cluster of German children were gathered on the piles of rubble outside the airfield fence and they scrambled to catch the packets of candy with their makeshift parachutes of handkerchiefs.

Neeley considered the tactical situation. Would the Shadow try to disrupt this smoothly running operation? Tunner had developed a complex, but efficient, system for staggering the aircraft into Tempelhof. A cargo plane took off from an airfield in West Germany every three minutes and flew 'stacked' in what was dubbed the 'ladder'. Three minutes apart and separated by five hundred feet of elevation from 4,000 feet to 6,000 feet, this conveyor belt worked nonstop, twenty-four hours a day. The crews were rotated every six hours.

Neeley remembered sitting in the log cabin in New Hampshire with Gant, her lover and a former Special Operations soldier. He'd taught her target analysis and Neeley applied those lessons to what was before her and in the download.

She shook her head. Shooting down a plane would be an act of war. The Russians were already trying harassing tactics such as fly by's, flashing searchlights at inbound planes and other tactics. None of it would prove effective.

Shut down radio communication? That would be crippling, Neeley knew as she checked the data. During limited visibility, radio was the only way the incoming flight could get on track to land. But the Allies had backups and were prepared for that. It would cause a delay, but not stop the airlift. Unless, Neeley thought, they misdirected traffic during bad weather, much like hacking into a GPS signal and shifting it. They could crash a number of planes in low visibility before the ruse was uncovered. That would be a significant setback, but would require a number of rogue transmitters.

The key chokepoint for the entire operation was maintenance. The aircraft required 25, 200 and 1,000 hour inspections, which took them off the line. But those didn't take place here and Neeley was here, at Tempelhof. Whatever the Shadow had planned would go down here.

Large lights clicked on all along the edge of the rooftop, illuminating the unloading area. Neeley looked about, the darkening grey sky reminding her of her years here, well after the war, but with the ever-present specter of the results. Especially among the older people who'd lived through it, the Russian invasion and then the Allied occupation.

During the latter stages of the war the Germans had used the terminal and hangers to put together aircraft after shipping the parts in from other parts of the country. The airfield had been taken by the Russians, who ransacked it, searching for anything of value. The Russians had destroyed whatever they found. One interesting aspect of Tempelhof was it was the first airport to have an underground railroad running the length of the terminal. When the Russians had come across a sealed steel bunker under one of the northern administrative buildings, they'd assumed something important was hidden behind it. They'd blown the door.

What that they hadn't known, nor bothered to learn from the survivors, was that the bunker contained Lufthansa's archives of celluloid film for aerial photography. The highly flammable material had ignited and burned for days. To solve the problem, the Russian commander had the lower levels of the airport flooded.

Interesting, Neeley thought, but what did that have to do with now? Edith tended to fill the downloads with everything she could get from the analysts. Neeley couldn't blame her, because no one knew what would end up being pertinent given Dane's 'vagaries of the variables'.

Neeley looked past the runway at what had once been a magnificent city, barely visible as night descended. Between American and English bombing, and then the final assault by the Russians, even now, three years after the war, it was mostly ruins. Later, when Neeley arrived here as a teenager, a good portion of it still wasn't rebuilt.

It was a broken, darkened skeleton of pre-war Berlin. Many streets were impassable because of debris. Edith's download scrolled a list of facts. Because there were so few men left in the city, it was the women doing the work. Not just shoveling coal out of cargo planes, which was actually a premier job since one worked for the Americans. Women and children of all ages were removing over two billion bricks, one by one. Most to be reused eventually in rebuilding. But before one could rebuild, the destruction had to be cleared away. A quarter of the women prostituted themselves to the occupiers, a step up from *Kom Frau.*

Hunger was the common denominator. Food was on everyone's mind. And with winter approaching it would be the bone-chilling wet cold. Neeley shivered from her own memories.

She continued watching the C-47's landing, one after another, on schedule. Alternating with the empty ones taking off. A precision operation amidst the ruins. When she'd lived here, she'd heard the admiration, the thanks, in the voices of the Berliners who's lived through this. Edith hadn't been far off in labeling it one of the finest moments in American history. To help a defeated enemy, especially one that had committed such atrocities against mankind.

"What are you doing, kraut?" An American NCO with a military police armband strode toward Neeley. He had a nightstick in hand and did not look happy to see her up here. "If you're on a work crew, get your ass downstairs."

"*Excuse me?*" Neeley replied in German.

"Don't speak that kraut crap to me," the sergeant said. He stopped three feet away and appraised her.

Neeley held up the letter. "I have authorization from General—"

The sergeant cut her off. "So you do speak English." He laughed. "Right. Like the general would be giving you a letter." His eyes narrowed in thought and he looked about, making sure no one else was on the roof. With his free hand he reached into his pocket and pulled out a candy bar. "How 'bout you and me make a trade? I'll give you this and won't report you for being in a restricted zone and you give me—"

He didn't finish as Neeley attacked, her fist aiming for his throat. She was surprised as he dodged the blow and jabbed her in the solar plexus with the nightstick, knocking the wind out.

Neeley dropped to her knees, gasping for breath. The MP's boot hit her in the chin with a snap kick, tumbling her onto her back. As she lay there, still trying to breathe, stunned from the kick, he placed the boot on her chest, pressing down where the baton had already hurt her.

"I was told you would be a worthy opponent." He drew a knife, the sharp steel glittering. "I am sad that is not true. I am Legion and you will die slowly and with much blood."

AREA 51

"You've changed things a bit," Ivar said, looking about. "I like the paint."

The steel-reinforced concrete walls were covered with red shellac and someone had done a nice job on one of the walls of sketching out a desert scene with the sun either rising or setting; given it was the Nightstalkers, most likely the latter. The ceiling had been scraped clean of the popcorn insulation which Ivar had hated. Above them, twenty feet of concrete protected the facility from a direct nuclear strike. There were a couple of doors: one leading to the team leader's CP—command post. Another to the armory, a third to the living quarters, and the fourth to the entrance to the room where the team leader and sergeant had met with the image of Mrs. Jones.

"Who's running things now?" Ivar asked.

"I'm the team leader," the man with the gun said. "Jace."

"Is that a girl's name?" Angus asked. "Do you fellas still do the naming thing? How'd you end up with that moniker?"

Jace ignored the comment.

Orlando indicated: "Angus and Ivar."

"Read about you," Jace said to Ivar. "You've been through a Rift."

"I've been through more than a Rift," Ivar said.

Several more armed personnel came out of the living quarters. Three men and two women. They all had the hard look that Ivar lacked, but Angus had in spades.

"He's Ivar," Jace told them. "And Angus." He looked at Angus. "And read about you too. Aren't you supposed to be in the Super-Max?"

"Out for good behavior," Angus said. "That's nice that you've read about us. I oft tell children that reading is good for them."

"Easy," Orland said. He turned to Angus and Ivar. "They're your backup."

"We're *what*?" Jace was incredulous.

Orlando ignored him.

"Backup means we be going into a wee spot of danger, I suppose?" Angus asked.

Orlando crooked a finger and led Angus and Ivar to a large video monitor. "Take a look." He typed into a laptop computer hooked to it.

The screen flickered then there was an image.

"What am I looking at?" Angus asked.

"The Can," Ivar said.

"That wasn't in the briefing book," Angus said.

"It's below the Archives at Area 51," Ivar said. "Moms mission is to the lab that was where the Archives are now. The Can is below that."

"What are you talking about? Backup?" Jace demanded as the other Nightstalkers gathered behind him.

Orlando turned and faced them. "You received your mission tasking correct? To do what I order you?"

"Yes, but—"

"No, buts, Jace," Orlando cut him off. "Stand by. You know what happened and these men need to get up to speed."

Ivar continued his explanation to Angus. "What you're looking at is below that. It took three years to build and cost a shitload of money. More than a new aircraft carrier."

"Aye," Angus agreed. "That's a dung-load. What's it do?"

"It's a Super-Kamiokande," Ivar said. "It detects muonic activity in the planet. There are three in the world. Only one is public knowledge; that's in Japan. We've got this one and the Russians have one."

The image showed several work stations set atop steel grating inside a wide, circular cavern.

"What's under the grating?" Angus asked. "It shimmers."

"Water," Ivar said. "Inside a stainless-steel tank. Sixty meters wide by sixty deep. The walls of the tank are lined with twenty thousand photomultiplier tubes. They're sensitive light sensors that can detect a single photon as it travels through the water and reacts with it. They're all linked together to those displays at the workstations."

"How come nobody's at work?" Angus asked.

Orlando answered that. "That's why you're here."

"Not sounding good," Angus muttered.

"The Can detects Rifts forming," Ivar explained. "Technically, it's a ring-imaging water Cerenkov detector. Cerenkov light is produced when an electrically charged particle travels through water. Being so far underground allows the earth and rock to block out the photons emitted by human devices on the surface of the planet. It also helps that we're in the middle of the desert."

"Righto," Angus said, his tone indicated what he thought of the explanation.

"You need to understand the scenario we're going into," Orlando chided him.

"'We'?" Angus said. "You'll be joining us?"

Orlando didn't reply and Ivar continued. "Just a couple of generations ago physicists thought the building blocks of matter were the proton, electron and neutron. They were aware of three other particles: the photon, neutrino and positron. But it didn't add up. They knew they were missing something. Protons near the nucleus, having equal charges, should repel each other. But they don't. The reason they don't is the meson. So scientists dug deeper. They found other particles. One was the pion."

"'Peon'?" Angus said.

"P-I-O-N," Ivar spelled out. "The other was the muon. Both are very unstable and when they're split, they decay fast." Ivar indicated the image of the Can. "The muon decays into an electron, a neutrino and an antineutrino. We don't know why, but whenever Rifts begin to form, they emit muons. And they don't decay naturally."

"Do Gates emit muons?" Angus asked.

"No," Ivar said. "That's why we've never been able to detect them."

"So Gates aren't just bigger Rifts?" Angus said.

Ivar shrugged. "They could be. The Can is focused into the planet. Since the planet doesn't emit charged particles, when it picks up muonic activity, that means a Rift is going to form. The Can gives thirty-eight minutes of warning." Ivar glanced at Jace. "When was the last one?"

"We've never had one," Jace sheepishly admitted. "Ever since the previous team, your old team, shut the one in Tennessee."

"That's why you're here," Orlando explained to Ivar. "We need some experience."

Ivar nodded. "That Rift was the one where Colonel Thorn and the Demon Core came back through."

"Ah," Angus said. "I did read about the poor colonel and his plane accident with all the Jap and Kraut scientists on board."

Orlando coughed as if clearing his throat. "The thing is, that first Rift occurred above the Can."

"Where Moms is," Angus said. "Except, you know, then."

Orlando glanced at the Nightstalkers who were hanging on every word. "Yes."

"Is there a connection to no one being at work?" Angus asked.

"Watch," Orlando said as he clicked the mouse.

Three people were in the Can's control center. Two were staring at screens, while the third was leaning back in his chair, stretching his arms. The screen flickered and they were gone.

"Time lapse?" Angus asked.

"No," Orlando said.

"What was the flicker?"

"We don't know," Orlando replied. "No Rift. No Gate. Something happened and they were gone in an instant."

"Has anyone been down there since?" Angus asked. He recognized the look that Orlando gave him. "Aye, then. I guess we'll be going about that, now, eh?"

"We've cleared out everyone from Area 51," Orlando said. "The Archives, Everyone inside Groom Mountain is out of the hangers. The airfield. Lots of unhappy people but given one of the missions is to Area 51 in the past at a critical juncture and this is happening now, we felt it best not to take chances."

"Who be this we?" Angus asked and was ignored.

Orlando pointed up. "Let's get moving. Time's a wasting."

THE MISSIONS PHASE III

NEW YORK CITY, 22 September 1776

Scout followed Montressor and Rogers out of the greenhouse. The latter stormed off away from the mansion while Montressor faced Scout. "Was there anything to what Rogers was saying, girl?"

Scout looked the Captain in the eyes. "No, sir. But the prisoner requested a Bible and no one has brought him one. I don't think that's—" Scout searched her vocabulary for the right word— "sporting."

"It's not very Christian, for certain," Montressor said. "Get him a Bible." He went up the wide front stairs of the house as the rising sun reflected off the windows on the east side of the house.

Scout started after him, then realized her position, here and now, and went around to the servant's entrance. As she did, she marveled at the undulating green countryside, a mixture of fields and forest, that would become Brooklyn across the East River. The download informed her that the boundary of New York City was actually well south of here on Manhattan Island, clustered around the tip. Large estates and farms covered portions of the island and there were still large tracts of virgin forest. Scout breathe deeply, savoring the fresh air.

What Montressor had said was true, the download confirmed. Rogers had come back from England in 1775 after petitioning the King for funds and being turned down. The petition had a solid basis in that Rogers had financed his Rangers for many years out of his own pocket. Of course, he'd also gambled away a considerable amount of money and invested in some failed enterprises as well as an arrest for counterfeiting. Rogers had also asked the King to be allowed to search for the famed Northwest Passage. That too had been denied. There were historians who speculated that if he'd been given the backing, that Rogers might have made it to the Pacific decades before Lewis and Clark.

Upon his return, the Committee of Safety formed by the Continental Congress had initially arrested Rogers on suspicion of spying for the Crown. They'd paroled him on his promise that he would not serve against the colonists. Later, in a seeming change of heart and considering his exploits in the French and Indian War, Congress had offered Rogers a commission in the army but he'd declined, saying he was a British officer. Except then, in another twist after a cold shoulder from the British, Rogers wrote Washington seeking a command in his army.

Scout entered the house as she pondered the flipflops in loyalty. Washington had not only refused Rogers a command, he'd had the man arrested. Rogers had escaped and was in the process of forming up a Ranger company at the moment, which he would employ against the Colonists.

The only person in the kitchen was the black cook, who was scrubbing the pots.

"Is there a Bible handy?" Scout asked her.

The cook looked at Scout and her eyes narrowed as if she saw something. "Be careful, girl. Rogers is a snake." She made the sign of the cross. "And you got the devil's aura around you but your soul seem pure. Be careful, girl." She pointed toward the dining room and went back to work.

Scout edged the door open, making sure the room was empty. She spotted a Bible open on a dresser—the download tried to intrude with the correct historical term for the piece of furniture, which of course was not dresser, and Scout pushed it away. *Really, Edith*? The Bible was propped open on a fancy wood stand which Scout was sure had some fancy official term that she didn't allow to download.

As she turned to leave, she heard voices in the next room. She edged up to the door and listened. She recognized General Howe's voice. And Major Roberts.

"It would be deceitful," Howe said.

"It is war, General."

"Your hatred of Washington has colored your views, Major."

"If you destroy Washington's army," Rogers said, "you crush the rebellion. They cannot replace him or the men. This is a time for bold action."

"Do not lecture me, Major." But there was little energy in Howe's voice.

"Your brother tried to negotiate peace with traitors, General," Rogers said.

"With the King's permission," General Howe said.

Scout knew about that: it had been Doc's mission on Nine-Eleven: the Staten Island Peace Conference just the previous week, which had been attended by Admiral Howe and Benjamin Franklin and John Adams. She thought it odd that Doc had been here, in this time, just 11 days ago and not far away. General Howe had not attended the meeting because he harbored a great resentment toward Benjamin Franklin, who had had an affair with the Howe's sister, Caroline, while in England and impregnated her.

"Despite our differences with the Colonists, peace would be preferable," General Howe said. "You as well as anyone should know that this war will not be easy and there is a very good chance, we may lose it. England is far away and our supply line is tenuous and long. The colonies cover too large an area for us to subdue."

"All the more reason to send Hale to Washington as I suggest," Rogers said. "Wouldn't peace on the King's terms be preferable? You don't need to wipe out his army. Minus Washington, they will fall apart. Trust me. I know these people. Without a leader like him, they have little spine for war. Their army is ragtag with little discipline."

"You were all for stringing Hale up right away yesterday," Howe said. "Why the change of heart?"

"You might say I've just had a heavenly vision, General," Rogers said.

Scout froze. That had to be Valkyries. What was Rogers planning? What was he going to change today and how would that lead to Washington's death, and possibly the destruction of his army?

"'A heavenly visit'?" Howe repeated. "I've warned you about your drinking, Major."

"Oh, this was real, General. Trust me."

"I don't trust you at all," Howe said.

"Let me put it another way, then, General. What do we have to lose with my plan? If Hale causes Washington to act as I believe he will, it gives you the perfect opportunity to surprise his army and destroy it. If my plan fails, nothing is lost."

"Except some honor."

"As *you've* noted, General. I have none to lose."

Scout hurried away as she heard footsteps approaching the door. She was through the kitchen.

Scout rushed back to the greenhouse, quickly reviewing the military situation in her mind. After successive defeats, the Battle of Harlem Heights north of here had been a little over a week ago on the 16th, with Washington winning his first fight of the war, but gaining no strategic advantage other than causing Howe to halt his troops in place on Manhattan. Eventually, after a month of nothing much, Washington would withdraw most of his army out of Manhattan leaving Fort Washington garrisoned on the northern tip. The Battle of White Plains would take place on the 28th of October when General Howe attempted to flank the Continental Army by landing farther up the Hudson. Washington had been warned though and withdrew to White Plains. The pitched battle caused Washington to retreat north and then across the Hudson to New Jersey. Fort Washington would be taken by the British on 16 November and both armies would pull back to quarter for the winter except for the surprise attack on the Hessians on the day after Christmas at Trenton.

How was Rogers going to use Nathan Hale to change that?

She displayed the Bible to the guard who allowed her entry. Hale was folding a letter and he inscribed it on the outside for the recipient: his mother.

"Here you are, sir," Scout said, offering the Bible.

"Thank you," Hale said as he took it. He smiled. "I am indeed blessed."

Scout found his attitude strange for a man who would be dead in an hour and a half; an abrupt change from not long ago. And strange meant she needed to dig. "How so, sir?"

Hale sat down, back to the orange tree, Bible in his lap. "When I was captured, I was terrified. Which is most natural for such a situation, I do believe. I knew what my fate would be. It is the rule of war for spies caught behind enemy lines. Most of the night I contemplated my doom. But just after you left this morning, I learned that my fear was for naught. That I should celebrate my sacrifice."

Scout sat down in front of him. "Will you tell me why?"

He held up the Bible. "My faith will see me through. It has already delivered more than I could have dreamed."

Thoughts and prayers. The words ran through Scout's brain but she didn't say them. "I'm glad your faith gives you comfort."

Hale leaned forward and lowered his voice. "I was told I would be saved."

Scout felt a familiar chill. "By whom?"

Hale shook his head. "And the prophecy was correct. After you left, Major Rogers came back. He told me that he will ensure that I will not die today. That I will be pardoned right before the order for my hanging, with the noose around my neck. That he truly does side with our righteous cause. That his heart is with the place of his birth, here, rather than England. He will ensure that I am allowed to go free. He gave me papers that he says must be delivered secretly to General Washington. The British plan of attack. When I am pardoned, he will escort me through British lines so I can go to Washington and warn him."

"Why would he do that?"

"That is the amazing part." Hale held up the Bible. "Rogers had the same visitor I did, who confirmed we are the righteous."

"Who was that?" Scout asked, but she already knew the answer.

"An angel directly from God."

Frak me, Scout thought. Valkyries.

She channeled her inner Lara: "Can I see these papers?"

Hale frowned. "Who exactly are you?"

"A patriot," Scout said. "A friend to the cause. In case something happens, I can warn Washington."

"I have Rogers' word," Hale said, but he reached inside his shirt and retrieved a narrow oilskin pouch. He unfolded it and drew out several pieces of parchment. It occurred to Scout that he hadn't learned his lesson about being covert from the previous day and his capture. He leaned close to Scout as he spread them out on the dirt. "The common perception in Washington's camp is that General Howe will continue to pursue him. Drive his forces out of northern Manhattan and up the Hudson. Split New England from the rest of the colonies. Seize West Point and choke off the river. But that is *not* what Howe plans."

But it is what Howe does, Scout thought. To an extent. She looked at the map and the arrows and the various British units designated to march and sail. Not north, but west and south.

Hale explained what she was seeing. "General Howe is going to split his army. Half on board ships under his brother's command to sail south and then up the Delaware River, while the General leaves a token defensive force to hold the city. He takes the rest of the army across the Hudson and strikes out for Philadelphia by land. The plan is to seize the city in a pincer movement and capture the Continental Congress. As deployed now, Washington's army is to the north and would be left behind if Howe moves swiftly."

It made sense except it wasn't what Howe was going to do. Scout saw the trap that Rogers was extending to Washington in the form of Hale delivering these papers. If Washington believed them, he would most likely move west, cross the Hudson and try to block the British Army from getting into New Jersey. But in doing so, he'd be abandoning his established defensive positions and opening his flank to an attack by Howe's entire army, not half, while on the move.

Scout realized she'd have to get to Washington with Hale and convince the General to not believe the plan. That was possible when Hale was spared the rope; that should make anyone suspicious.

Or.

Scout would have to make sure Nathan Hale died, one way or another.

. . .

SALEM, MASSACHUSETTS. 22 September 1692

"Your friends are here," Pandora said.

"I don't think they've come for a group hug," Lara said. She noted that each of the Lukas had a dagger in hand.

"Are you going to join your brothers?" Pandora asked.

"No. I'm going to kill them, most likely."

"If so," Pandora said, "perhaps they're here to test you?"

"I don't know why they're here," Lara said, "but it ain't for a good reason." Then she detected Unity Hale. The young girl was in the forest, alone, but returning. The three Lukas were between her and the girl. Lara moved away from the village, toward the, *was the plural of Lukas, Luki* and she wondered why she would think that? Was it part of Edith Frobish's download or older, something in her origin?

The three were identical, which they should be since they were grown in a vat. Superb genetics leading to wide shoulders, flat stomachs, well-muscled late teens on the verge of manhood. Their skin was pale, not enough sun in the vat, Lara supposed. They wore dark slacks and shirts. Black, curly hair that she envied. Why had the males been given the good hair? She'd have to take that up with management.

When, and if, she ever met management, she supposed there might be bigger issues to discuss.

"Let's take it out of town, boys," Lara said. "Everyone's getting a good night of sleep before the morning's show."

The center Lukas, whom Lara dubbed Lukas2, going from left to right, not that she was going to be able to keep track of them, swept his hand, inviting her into the forest. "Certainly."

"Coming?" Lara asked Pandora. "Or sitting this one out? I'll give you back your stick."

"What do you think is going to happen once you go in there?" Pandora asked.

"They'll probably try and kill me," Lara said.

"What if they're here to meet you?"

"I didn't bring my secret decoder ring," Lara said. "We won't have much to discuss."

"You think you know whose side you're on," Pandora said. "But the best operatives are those who don't know they're an operative. Who think they're doing a good thing. For a long time you had no idea who you were, correct? Why do you think you do now?"

Before Lara could respond, Pandora stepped back and disappeared through a gate.

"Great," Lara muttered. "What happened to 'she is one of us' about Unity?"

She strode forward, Naga staff in one hand, dagger in the other.

The Lukas triangulated Lara as she walked deeper into the woods. She was trying to keep track of them while keeping tabs on Unity's aura. The young girl was approaching, but slowly, as if she were taking a leisurely stroll in the dark woods. However, her aura was agitated, distraught over something, which made sense, given pending events.

Maybe my pending death, Lara thought as she stopped short of the clearing she'd arrived in. She saw no point in giving the Lukas trio an open field of battle. Lara slowly turned in a circle next to the thick trunk of a towering oak tree. The three were spaced evenly about. She imagined that if she measured, they would be perfect points on an equilateral triangle.

"What do you boys want?" she called out.

"To talk," one replied.

"Why the daggers in hand, then?"

"This is a dangerous place and time," the same one answered.

"You guys got names, cause you look alike to me."

"You do not look like the Lara's we've seen before," one replied.

"It's the hair, right? You like what I've done with it?"

"It's more than the hair. We are all Lukas. But you are not all Lara."

"You guys sure know how to chat a girl up," Lara said. They were keeping their distance, but Unity was getting closer. "What do you want to talk about?"

"We did not say it was you we desired to talk to," a Lukas replied.

"Frak me," Lara exclaimed, caught flat-footed, as all three sprinted off, directly toward Unity.

Time slowed for Lara as she ran through the forest, avoiding trees, brambles and 'wait-a-minute' vines that reached out to trip. She could see clearly, not quite as if daylight, but well enough. The Lukas trio was dark red outlines spread out ahead of her. And beyond them, was Unity's troubled aura, pulsing dark green.

Unity must has sensed them coming because she suddenly dashed to the side.

The adjustment in course allowed Lara to close on the farthest left Lukas. He was twenty feet in front of her, angling across. Then fifteen. He became aware of her and abruptly turned toward her, a delaying force.

Lara's fury accelerated her and she slammed into the Lukas before either had a chance to bring their weapons up. The impact left them both stunned, but Lara was quicker to recover. She sprang to her feet and jabbed the Naga staff toward him. He rolled, avoiding the thrust, scrambling, shaking his head to clear it, knife hand at the ready.

"No!" Lara screamed. She slashed with the Naga staff, separating hand from body.

Lukas' eyes grew wide, then he reached with his surviving hand for the blade on the forest floor. Lara pinned it, thrusting the point of the Naga through the hand into the dirt. With her other hand, she slammed the dagger up, into his jaw, ripping into the brain.

The body turned to dust before she could pull the dagger out.

She continued her pursuit, but the delaying tactic had worked, costing her valuable seconds.

Unity had stopped and the two Lukas were closing in on her, albeit at a slower pace.

Lara arrived, finding the two Lukas facing a massive boulder that was cracked in the center. And in the crack, her back to the crevice, was Unity. She had both hands up, one toward each of the Lukas and oddly, both seemed to be struggling to get to her. Pushing forward as if against an invisible force, moving in extreme slow motion.

Lara didn't waste time figuring it out. She decapitated the Lukas on the left with one sweep of the Naga. Head and body crumbled into dust. The other turned toward her, raising his blade in defense, but much too slowly, as she slammed the blood-coated blade into his chest, through the heart. She twisted, shredding. The last Lukas was dust to dust.

WASHINGTON D.C.. 22 September 1862

Eagle felt like part of the furniture, standing unnoticed by the fireplace as Mary Todd sobbed in her husband's arms. The Keep had leaned back in her wheelchair, letting this wind down. But Mary Todd was only partly placated. She pulled back from her husband's embrace. "Will you do as I ask?"

"It's just an announcement," Lincoln protested.

"It will inflame many," Mary Todd said. "There are hotheads here in Washington who will take affront. Whose anger will boil over."

"It will not take effect until the first of the next year," Lincoln said. "There will be plenty of time to deal with the naysayers and for the fires of dissent to diminish."

"Not if you are dead." Mary Todd put a claw-like hand on the

President's shoulder. "We must have peace. There is too much blood. Slavery will eventually be abolished. It will come in stages. As they did it in New York. A progression."

"Sir?" the Keep said to the President. "It has arrived. This morning."

Lincoln nodded, but his focus was on Mary Todd.

The Keep pressed, but her voice was low-key. "What do you think of my idea?"

Lincoln frowned. "It might work."

"It will work, sir." The Keep spoke with a quiet urgency.

Mary Todd seized on the exchange. "What secrets do you keep from me? What communication do you whisper behind my back?"

"Just the business of the office," Lincoln said to her, but his mind was elsewhere now that the Keep had updated him.

Lincoln and Eagle were startled as Mary Todd's hand snaked out and she slapped the Keep on the cheek. She brought the hand back to hit again, but her husband grabbed it. "Stop it!" he ordered. He lowered his voice as he gently let go of her hand. "I know this is hard, my dear wife. But we must see the course."

"I did not want this! I did not want this house. This burden."

Lincoln raised an eyebrow in disbelief but she didn't see it. He sighed. "I must get back to the office." He stood. "Perhaps you should rest?" he suggested to his wife. He didn't wait for an answer as his wife threw herself back on the couch.

Lincoln departed through the door he'd entered.

"Get out," Mary Todd snarled at the Keep. "Get out."

The Keep looked over her shoulder at Eagle. "Take me to my office."

Eagle got behind the wheelchair and headed for the door. As they left, he glanced back at Mrs. Lincoln. She was staring straight ahead, face expressionless.

As Eagle pushed, the Keep asked him. "Are you here to help Mrs. Lincoln?"

"I'm here to ensure the Proclamation is announced," Eagle said.

"Of course, you would want that," the Keep said. "But what of Mrs. Lincoln?"

Her life is misery and will only get worse, Eagle thought, but did not say. "She will persevere."

"You are here for the President, then?"

"It is a momentous day," Eagle said. "Today, the President will announce the Proclamation."

"The Proclamation can wait. The President needs his wife."

"The Proclamation cannot wait."

"Why? It will make no difference as the President said. It will not go into effect until next year. And it has no teeth."

Eagle got her in the office and followed, shutting the door behind. "But it will happen today."

"He has been reconsidering."

"Why?" Eagle asked.

"He knew of the Declaration from the Book of Truths," the Keep said. "I reminded him of it and told him I was making an attempt to have it recovered."

"It changes nothing."

"The President is wise enough to understand why this Declaration wasn't made public in 1776 and again in 1826. Even by one of your own people, who had a stake in it. That would cause anyone to reconsider."

"Has he read it?"

"Not yet," the Keep said. "It was delivered just before you arrived."

"From where?"

"Monticello, of course."

A quick dip into the download. "That's well behind Confederate lines."

"Many pass through the lines in either direction," the Keep

said. "On all sorts of missions. It was not hard to find someone to accomplish the task." The Keep pointed at him. "Who exactly are you? Where do you, and your comrades in the past, come from? Perhaps it is better if I ask *when* you come from?"

Given the stakes, Eagle felt an urge to tell her. She did, after all, keep the Book of Truths, which meant she could keep a secret. And the president in the future, in his time, would be aware of the Time Patrol. What wasn't in the download was which president was informed of its existence. One thing for certain: it wasn't in his mission mandate and Rule One of the Time Patrol was pre-eminent.

"My people have their own form of the Book of Truths," Eagle said. "It's an oral tradition. It is said that today is the day when President Lincoln will announce the Emancipation Proclamation. It must happen as it is foretold."

The Keep put a shaking hand on her book. "My book is of lessons learned and what has happened. How can you have a story of what *will* happen?"

Fighting the desire to tell the truth, Eagle belatedly checked the download for information on the Keep, this particular Keep, but there was nothing. That had been compartmentalized completely, passed from one woman to the next. Always a woman.

"Please tell me," the Keep begged. "Help me understand. I will not write of it in the Book."

"My people have seers," Eagle hedged. "Women who can see things. Sometimes they catch glimpses of the future."

"Witches?"

"No," Eagle said, as he thought of Lara and her mission. "They are real. They have a certain power that is passed down through generations to a handful of people."

"Curious," the Keep said. "And one of them has told you that this must happen today?"

"That's what is foretold."

"I sense you are withholding," the Keep said. She smiled. "But sometimes secrets are important, are they not?"

"They are," Eagle said.

The Keep indicated the door. "If what you say is true, we should talk to the President. Be warned, though, that it will take more than just a story to convince him of anything. Besides, he will want to see the Declaration."

They headed toward Lincoln's office in the southeast corner of the top floor of the White House. It was up here that Lincoln worked and also held cabinet meetings. Edith, thorough as usual, informed him via the download that the Oval Office was not yet in existence; it would be built in 1909 by President Taft. Until then, the living quarters and offices were mixed on the second floor of the main building of the White House.

The door to Lincoln's office was cracked open and the Keep knocked.

"Come in, come in," Lincoln called out.

The Keep pushed the door wide and Eagle rolled her in.

"Shut the door behind, please," Lincoln ordered. He was standing by a window, staring out. The walls were covered with dark green wallpaper and floor covered with a carpet of the same color, making the room moody and dark. Numerous military maps were pinned to the walls. A desk was submerged in paper; newspapers, petitions from office seekers and all sorts of correspondence. There seemed to be no organization to it but one got the sense everything was exactly where the man wanted it to be.

Lincoln didn't turn to face them as he spoke. "Is that the document you spoke of?"

"Yes, Mister President," the Keep said. "The original Declaration of Emancipation."

Eagle was tempted to speak up, but he decided to wait, to see how this played out.

Lincoln pointed with a long finger, still looking out the

window as if he didn't want to face the responsibility inside. "Put it on that chair, if you will."

The Keep did so.

Eagle couldn't see past the President but he knew what the nation's capitol looked like now. The Washington Memorial was just a stub, stalled in construction due to a lack of funds. Work was slowly proceeding on the Capitol Dome at Lincoln's insistence, despite the war. Troops were quartered everywhere, with tents spread out on every piece of ground that wasn't occupied by live-stock to feed those troops.

Lincoln turned. "Your Book has been helpful," he acknowl-edged to the Keep. "Knowing the true thoughts of the men who came before me, unvarnished and rough, cuts away the façade of the office and the politicking. The pretense we must uphold that we, who bear the responsibility for the Republic, actually know what we're doing." He chuckled. "There are days I truly wonder why anyone would want this burden on their shoulders." He picked up the wooden tube and pulled out the stopper on the end. "From Jefferson's slave's own hand, eh?"

"It was most likely buried by Thomas Jefferson's own hand."

"He did not speak of this woman in the Book," Lincoln noted as he removed a piece of parchment, yellowed with age. "One can tell, reading between the lines, that he was a tight man with his emotions. Intriguing, given he had the greatest talent with the pen this country has ever seen."

Eagle spoke. "The head and the heart, sir. President Jefferson always yielded to the head."

"Ah, you are not mute," Lincoln said. He had the document in hand but had not unrolled it. "The head and the heart. So, you are a literate man? You've read Jefferson's letters?"

"Yes, sir," Eagle replied. "He argued the head and the heart over his affair with Mrs. Cosway. 12 October 1786."

"'Affair'?" Lincoln shook his head. "A strong word. I'm afraid I only perused that particular missive and don't recall it exactly. Which won? The head or the heart?"

"The head, sir," Eagle said, sensing that Lincoln remembered it quite well. "After all, Jefferson did not ask her to come from Paris to Monticello. But he did bring Sally Hemings back. Although slavery had been abolished in France and she could have petitioned for her freedom and remained."

Lincoln raised a bushy eyebrow. "Curious. I was not aware of that. Why did she turn down her opportunity at freedom?"

"She was pregnant with Mister Jefferson's child, sir," Eagle said.

"But he didn't acknowledge it," Lincoln pointed out. "Why not take freedom?"

"With what means, sir?" Eagle asked.

Lincoln nodded. "You bring up a point which is looming. For a Negro, you have quite a bit of information others consider terrible rumors about a great man."

"Many of Jefferson's records in this regard were destroyed or manipulated," Eagle said. "That particular child died shortly after their return to the United States."

"There were more?" Lincoln asked.

"There were, sir."

"I've not seen you in the house before," Lincoln said.

"He's a new hire, sir," the Keep replied.

"He is quite forward for a servant," Lincoln observed. "Where did you learn to read?"

"It does not matter, sir," Eagle said.

"A negro learned in letters is a rare commodity," Lincoln said. "And one so widely read and full of knowledge even more so. It seems one would have a better task than wheeling an old woman around?"

"We each have our missions in life, Mister President," Eagle said. "Today, this is mine."

Lincoln unrolled the Declaration and scanned it. "Amazing. And it *is* signed by the delegates. Not all, from a cursory glance, but enough it could have been law at the time."

Eagle spoke before the Keep could say anything. "The Committee of Five dared not present it with the Declaration of Independence to be enacted or else certain delegates would not have signed either Declaration. The compromise was that it would be put aside for fifty years."

The Keep cut in. "But it was not made public in 1826, Mister President. For very good reasons as we've discussed."

Lincoln rolled the Declaration of Emancipation and placed it back in the tube. He put it on top of a stack of newspapers. He faced Eagle. "You know this how? It was not in the Book that Mister Jefferson started."

Eagle weighed how to act. "My people have their own history, sir. We pass it orally from generation to generation. Sally Hemings, Mister Jefferson's slave, passed along her knowledge. I have had it passed to me from one who heard it directly from Hemings own lips before she passed on. It matches what is in the Book of Truths."

"The visitors?" Lincoln asked. "The one who appeared in 1776, foretelling the one who would be at Jefferson's deathbed as Hemings told the Keep in 1826?"

"That was part of it, sir."

"Why didn't this Hemings woman unearth that document in 1826 as had been agreed?"

"President Jefferson died on that day, sir," Eagle said. "It was his burden, not hers."

"And he let it slip," Lincoln noted. "He would not have done that lightly." His voice dropped. "Nothing is done lightly in this office."

Eagle reached into his pocket and pulled out a piece of purple cloth shaped like a heart with the word MERIT sewn on it. It was edged with lace. "One of my predecessors received this from General Washington himself during a discussion."

Eagle thought it was a reasonable lie, given he'd been the one to face Washington in 1783 in Newburgh.

"What is that?" Lincoln asked.

"An award General Washington had made up for soldiers who'd served gallantly, particularly enlisted soldiers. One of my group was given it by Washington at the Newburgh encampment in 1783."

"Let me see," Lincoln said.

Eagle walked around the Keep's chair, to the President, and extended the badge.

Lincoln examined it. "I've never seen the like. It certainly seems old enough." He handed it back, not as impressed as Eagle would have hoped.

The download informed Eagle that the badge had fallen into disuse after the Revolution and the Purple Heart, the distant descendant of it, would not be revived until 1932 as the Purple Heart medal.

"You are telling me," Lincoln said, "that there is a secret group of Negro historians with an oral tradition dating back to General Washington?"

"Before that even, sir," Eagle said. "General Washington listened to the member of our group on the 15th of March in 1783. Which is why he was given the Badge of Merit. Washington was considering traveling to Philadelphia to address the Continental Congress on the matter of lack of pay for officers and soldiers. A mutiny was brewing among his officers. Instead, the General made a speech that quieted the dissent."

The caught Lincoln's attention. "Ah yes!" He closed his eyes. *"'You will, by the dignity of your conduct, afford occasion for posterity to say, when speaking of the glorious example you have exhibited, had this day wanting, the world has never seen the last stage of perfection to which human nature is capable of attaining'."*

He'd gotten a few words off, but had captured the essence of the end of Washington's speech. "Yes, sir."

Lincoln indicated the tube. "I don't think Mister Jefferson let that slip. He knew in 1776 and just as well in 1826 that it would precipitate the rebellion we are now fighting." Lincoln walked to a chair and sank down in it. "But perhaps that would have been a good thing. There weren't as many of our fellow Americans to kill back then. And it would have been dealt with, not left to their descendants."

"Perhaps, sir," Eagle said. "But there are many possibilities. Sally Hemings didn't feel the country was ready for it. That the correct side would prevail."

"Who is to say the correct side will prevail now?" Lincoln mused. "Antietam was an awful battle and Robert Lee is far from licked. It is sad that someone who postures so nobly as Lee, fights for a cause so terrible. I wish he had accepted my offer of the Army. Antietam took place on Union soil. We are doing our best to twist the awful carnage into a victory, but neither side can claim that. This war is a long way from being over."

"You will prevail, sir," Eagle said.

"You sound certain," Lincoln said. "Are you a man of faith?" He didn't wait for an answer. "Now that we are in it, perhaps it would be best to do as you suggest—" here he indicated the Keep—" and release this document from men long dead rather than that I have drawn up? It would diffuse responsibility. Put the onus on those people in the South to refute what their own ancestors agreed to and, obviously, reneged on, although its doubtful any alive now are aware of it. But it would give us time. It was blessed by the delegates, both north and south."

"By a different government, sir," Eagle said.

"Who *exactly* are you?" Lincoln demanded.

"I represent the people who have had no voice, sir," Eagle said. "Sally Hemings and millions of other who have helped make this country what it is, but have borne the weight of slavery." Eagle knew that Frederick Douglas had not yet met the President. Here was a man fighting a war who had no counselor or advisor from the very people the war was about.

Lincoln's tone became cold. "Why are you here?"

"Today you are announcing the Emancipation Proclamation, sir," Eagle said. "It is a momentous occasion for my people."

"That is not certain," the Keep interjected. She turned to the President, her voice pleading. "Mister President, please take your wife's advice? As you can see from the evidence I have brought, the Committee of Five, brilliant men, realized the danger of Emancipation. We are now enmeshed in a brutal war. Ending that as quickly as possible should be our focus. Emancipation can come later."

Eagle felt the earnestness of her request, but he reminded himself of the history. "Sir, today is the day that—"

Lincoln cut him off. "Unless I decide *not* to announce it today. My wife, as you have seen, fears for my safety if I do so. There are some in my cabinet and many in the Congress who will not be pleased with it. I need their support to prosecute the war. Most of all, I need the support of the people."

"And then, sir," Eagle continued, "you will sign it into law in this very room on the First of January, next year."

"I will, eh?" He wagged a finger at Eagle. "You are most forward for a negro. For *anyone* coming into my office. You have not told me your name and you claim knowledge of things you should not know about." He pointed at the Keep. "Who is he?"

"He only arrived today, Mister President," the Keep said. "We have not had a chance to discuss matters."

"Arrived from where?" Lincoln asked.

"I don't know," the Keep said, joining him in staring at Eagle.

"Secrecy," Eagle said, "is how my people have managed to survive all these years. We have to stay in the shadows. There are many who would stamp us out ruthlessly if they learned of our existence."

"But you pop out of the shadows at rare moments and harass the President? To what end?"

"To ensure things are as they should be, sir."

"Yes, yes," Lincoln said, "but your arrogance in believing you know the correct path is outrageous and insulting."

"I mean no insult, sir," Eagle said.

"I was considered a decent lawyer in my younger days and I mixed with a wide cast of characters. I could always tell when someone was spinning me a yarn. I've been known to spin one or two myself."

"I cannot tell you the truth, Mister President," Eagle said.

Lincoln waved a hand of dismissal. "Of course not. It is what all story-tellers say when they have been found out. Emancipation has a larger purpose. I do not believe in slavery. It is an abomination, but I wish we could have worked it out peacefully with the southern states. Westward expansion and the nature of our government, of power, made it a powder-keg that grew larger and larger with every compromise. We were not heading in the correct direction. The only reason I've gotten the support I have for Emancipation is the fear of a foreign power involving itself in our war. This is between Americans, but there are those in England and France who sense opportunity. Who would rather deal with two countries at each other's throats than a united, powerful one across the Atlantic. Emancipation would make their involvement morally untenable."

"Yes, sir, it would," Eagle said. "But at its heart, it will do something no one has done before." Eagle pointed at the tube. "You are doing what they were afraid to."

"They had good reasons to be afraid," Lincoln said. He stood and went to the desk. He pulled a key from the waist coat pocket of his black coat. Opened the drawer on the lower left side of the desk. "You may have read considerably," Lincoln said as he pulled out a leather binder, "but you have not read what I have here. Only a select few have."

Eagle accessed the download but it came up with nothing relevant.

"It is from Jefferson Davis," Lincoln said. "A truce proposal with the lure of a staged rollback of slavery."

"It is the path you should seriously consider, sir," the Keep said. "The Proclamation would be a definitive no to that path without it even being explored. At the very least, the announcement can be postponed."

The download had nothing, which means the proposal had been destroyed and no words of it had ever leaked or else Edith would have tracked it down. There was information about a peace delegation later in the war *after* the Emancipation Proclamation made the possibility of European involvement on the Southern side impossible.

"As my wife suggested," Lincoln said, "Davis is using the example set by New York for the gradual elimination of slavery and the granting of freedom. He recommends that the rebelling states eventually rejoin the Union on a case by case basis. And this newly uncovered document would give the European countries pause." Lincoln held the letter in one hand and the tube with the Declaration of Emancipation in the other. "It seems I have a dilemma." He put both down. "I think it best to wait."

MANCHESTER, NEW YORK. 22 September 1823

Roland was carrying three, large gold plates as he followed Lachesis through the Gate. As he stepped through, it did finally occur to him to wonder why he was listening to her and whether he was abandoning his mission? The fact that she'd frozen Joseph Smith and the Valkyries, however, argued that her power was to be respected and perhaps, also, her knowledge.

She was a Fate after all.

They weren't Gods, at least that was the consensus on the Time Patrol, but they weren't people either. At least in the normal sense. The Naga passing through her indicated she wasn't really here, although she was here. Perhaps a hologram? Which reminded Roland that they'd always thought Mrs. Jones who'd headed the Nightstalkers was a hologram since no one from the team had met her face to face.

Lachesis could also summon Gates to wherever and whenever she wanted to do, which indicated great power. Roland figured he had nothing to lose by going along with her.

His musings were cut short as he was in the tunnel of time. The positive of being in the tunnel was that the plates had no weight. The walls were dark, no indication of other possibilities but perhaps that only happened when a mission was over? So far, everything on Roland's timeline should be the same, at least in regard to his mission, since it was on pause.

Or was he in a fold of time, Roland wondered, which was a rather starling insight for Roland.

They popped out of the Gate in a strange place. Red, rippled land stretched to the horizon in all directions, not a tree or blade of grass in sight. The moon was bright overhead.

"Where are we?" Roland asked, the three gold sheets tucked under one arm, the Naga ready in his other hand.

"The same place we were," Lachesis responded. "The same time. The same day. The same year."

"Huh?"

"Different timeline," Lachesis explained.

"How can that be? Where are the trees?"

"Things went a bit differently here."

"How—" Roland began but his question was interrupted by a dozen figures rising up, their red cloaks excellent camouflage with the terrain. They were armed with an assortment of spears, swords and bows. Two of the latter were notched and drawn and aimed at Roland.

Lachesis spoke a language that was indecipherable for Roland, even with all the tongues Edith put in the download. Four men appeared, two each on a pole, a similar stone case supported between them. They brought it forward and put it on the ground in front of the Fate. They removed the lid. It held twenty gold plates.

Lachesis closed her eyes and touched each plate in order. Then she opened her eyes and stepped back.

"Roland," Lachesis called out. She crooked a finger and he joined her. With her rod she tapped one of the plates inside the stone. "Replace this with that first plate you have." Roland did as ordered. She indicated two more to be replaced.

A Gate opened behind Lachesis. "Come along, Roland."

With three different gold plates, Roland dutifully followed. They went through the Gate and into a time tunnel. They stepped out onto a verdant hillside covered with towering trees under a clear night sky.

"Same place, same time?" Roland asked. "Different timeline?"

"Yes," Lachesis replied.

"What are we doing?"

"You wouldn't understand," Lachesis said as she peered about.

"Is this my mission?" Roland said. "Are they still frozen back in my timeline?"

"You ask many questions," Lachesis said.

"You don't explain much."

"Why should I?"

"You've asked me for help," Roland said. "It would be polite."

Lachesis laughed. "The fate of worlds is at stake and you're concerned about politeness."

Roland went on alert. "We're being watched."

"Of course, we are," Lachesis said. She called out in a different language Roland didn't understand.

An old man dressed in a well-worn leather shirt embroidered with brightly colored shells walked out from beneath the trees, one hand held up, palm showing. His skin was bronze, his dark hair long and straight and streaked with grey. He replied to her in the same language.

He spoke with Lachesis for a few moments, at one point indicating Roland. Whatever the Fate said satisfied him because he turned and shouted an order. Four younger men carried a stone sarcophagus into the clearing and removed the lid.

Lachesis repeated her procedure, running her hands over the plates. She tapped one. "Roland. Replace this one with the middle one you're carrying."

He did as instructed. "Who are these people?"

"What your timeline calls Native Americans," Lachesis said. "Except in this timeline, settlers from other lands have not arrived in the Americas. Naturally, the two continents aren't called the Americas either, but it's a long story, as the history of a timeline always is."

"Are you from a timeline?" Roland asked Lachesis as he finished swapping out the plate.

Lachesis peered at him in the moonlight. "Yes."

"So, you're human?"

"In a manner of speaking." She dismissed any further questions with a brusque wave of her hand. "We have several more timelines to visit and our time is short. Come."

"I got a mission," Roland said.

"You're doing it," Lachesis said. "This touches on your teammates' missions. Some of them at least."

"How?"

"You wouldn't understand."

Roland growled, but followed her. They went through the tunnel of time and stepped out of a gate into a disaster. The trees were blasted and torn; the earth scorched. Fires raged all about. Lachesis held up her rod and she and Roland were in a safe bubble amidst the ruin.

"Too late," Lachesis murmured. "Too late."

"I thought time was frozen?" Roland said.

"Only your timeline," Lachesis said.

Roland looked up, but the night sky was blocked by thick smoke. "The entire planet like this?"

Lachesis didn't respond. She opened another gate. "Come. Hurry. The Shadow has caught on."

They were through and the next timeline was very different. A hillside, but the spot they arrived at was part of a courtyard surrounded by a chest high marble wall. A tall man dressed in bright armor, a long sword strapped to his side, stood in front of them. Arrays behind him were two dozen knights in armor, albeit not as fine as his. They had helmets on, while their leader had his in the crook his arm, revealing a craggy face and long, dark hair. The sarcophagus was in front of him, lid already off.

As soon as they all saw Lachesis, they went to one knee, heads bowed.

Lachesis called out in another foreign tongue. The knights remained kneeling while the leader stood and spread his hands over the gold plates, his intent obvious. Lachesis checked them.

"I must think," she murmured to herself. "Things have changed." She touched each one and then ordered Roland to replace two.

"Good to go?" Roland asked when he finished.

"Not good," Lachesis said. "Sufficient. I hope. Come," she ordered and led the way to another gate.

When they were in the tunnel, Roland asked: "You're not going to explain any of this, are you?"

"You really wouldn't understand," Lachesis said.

"Try me. The Shadow is using those plates to send information how to open Rifts to the timelines, right?"

Lachesis spared him a glance. "Who thought of that?"

"We ain't as stupid as you think."

"Hmm." Lachesis sighed. "The plates are copies, not the originals. Corrupted copies made by the Shadow. Yes, there is information on Rifts. That is also corrupted, what word should I use? Dogma? Enough to send humans off on a twisted path."

"What's the straight path?" Roland asked.

Lachesis ignored the question as they exited the tunnel through another Gate.

AREA 51. 22 September 1947

Moms stifled the desire to tell the scientists to cease. They were checking various wires from the cart the Demon Core was on, to the arch and to the huge computers along the walls of the cavern. The processing power of each of those was probably less than a cell phone but it would be enough, combined with the atomic power of the Demon Core, to open the first Rift.

Moms knew the basics of shutting a Rift and the details were in the download, but she didn't have the equipment the Nightstalkers had used. She shouldn't need to do that, though, as the secret history of Area 51 recorded that the Rift was closed.

Eventually.

The issue was figuring out the wild card the Shadow was going to toss into this event. Moms walked closer, getting a better idea of the set-up, since the debrief would require it. The records of what exactly happened in here were vague, the few survivors having been more concerned about destroying the objects the Fireflies had taken over and closing the Rift.

It occurred to Moms, as she looked around, while she scanned the download, that no one in the debrief in 1947 had claimed responsibility for actually shutting the Rift. It appeared that the Rift had actually collapsed after sucking in the scientists, Colonel Thorn and some of his men, and, most significantly, the Demon Core. That made sense if the Core was the power behind opening the Rift. When it went through, the power would be gone.

It suddenly occurred to her that Thorn, in her present, actually her real past, had shown no signs of recognizing her when he came back through with the Demon Core. Of course, he, and the scientists, had also shown no sign of aging. They'd gone to someplace that had sounded very much like the Space Between. For them, little time had passed between now and then, decades in the future.

It was more than enough to give one a headache and she dismissed it. No one, except Thorn, paid her any attention. She caught snippets of Japanese, German and heavily accented English. There were Americans among the group. Some of them had worked on the Manhattan Project and were excited about what they were developing, even though they really had no idea of the powers they were delving into.

Moms walked the perimeter of the cavern clockwise. A man in a white coat was standing next to a table, looking at schematics and then the set up under the arch. Moms edged closer to see. He sensed her presence and turned. "Who are you?" He had a midwestern accent. Tall with sandy hair, he asked the question with a smile. "I'm sorry, I didn't mean to be rude."

"I've never seen those diagrams," Moms replied. "Where'd they come from?"

"Answering a question with a question is what the spooks around here do. Are you a spook?"

"I'm an observer."

"I'm Tim Jordan," he said, extending his hand. "My friends call me Jordie."

"Kate," Moms said, using the name on the documents provided by Support. She snapped off the download trying to dump information about Tim Jordan and his fate. She did notice he had deep blue eyes which reminded her of someone she'd didn't want to be reminded of.

"I've never seen you down here before," Jordan said. "Actually I've never seen a woman here. Not that I blame you. I try to stay as far as possible. But this—" he indicated the arch and then the drawing. "I had to be here."

"These schematics are pretty advanced," Moms said.

"I'd say they're out of this world," Jordan said, half-joking.

"What do you mean?"

"You haven't seen the original?

Moms shook her head.

Jordan checked his watch. "We've got a little time. Come on." He led her to a heavy steel door. He swung it open and turned on the lights inside a vault. On a table, propped up with a metal frame, was a thin golden plate with hieroglyphics on it.

"No one will say where it came from," Jordan said. "I don't think they know. But if you look at it closely, and believe me, we have, you can see quite a bit of advanced physics hidden among the crazy gobbly-gook."

Had Roland failed? Was Moms first thought. There was no mention of a gold plate in the download, and Edith had access to the Area 51 archives. Was this an anomaly caused by a failure in the current mission in 1823?

"Weird, huh?" Jordan asked, sensing her shock.

"Yes. Yes, it is," Moms managed. "I hadn't heard of this."

"Like everything here, top secret, Q-Clearance, hush-hush and all that. They only showed it to me when I got authorization, so if this is your first trip, you're in the same boat. You certainly came on the right day." He led her to exit, turning off the lights.

They entered the chamber.

"Colonel Thorn must be especially worried about this test," Jordan said.

"Why's that?" Moms asked, still trying to understand why a gold plate that was obviously what Sin Fen had mentioned being moved in the Space Between was here, now.

Jordan pointed. "Because he's got that down here. It's armed and he's got the control."

In a corner of the cavern was a large, black, football shaped object. Ten and a half feet long, five feet in diameter at its widest was Fat Man; an atomic bomb, brother to the one dropped on Nagasaki.

BERLIN, 22 September 1948

"I thought they would send the warrior Roland on this mission," Legion said, "Not a woman. But a woman can bleed and suffer as much as a man."

Neeley did a leg sweep, which Legion easily hopped over.

"Get to your feet," Legion ordered. "This is hardly worth the effort."

Neeley got to her knees, bending forward at the waist and grunting in apparent pain.

"Stand," Legion ordered.

Neeley got up, one hand sliding inside her coat for the M1911 while the other was held up, palm open. "Please, don't hurt me."

As she whipped out the pistol, Legion was in tight, good for the knife, bad for a gun. He grabbed her wrist and squeezed. Neeley heard and felt a bone break and she dropped the pistol. Legion shoved her away, against the waist high wall on the edge of the roof. Neeley almost fell over it, but caught herself, feeling the pain from the broken bone resonate up her arm.

Legion picked up the gun and stuck it in his web belt. "There is little honor to such weapons. You are not worth the blade." He strode toward Neeley and she knew he was going to shove her over the edge from the darkness on the roof onto the lit tarmac below.

She brought her hands up, shifting her feet, one slightly forward, ready to fight.

Four feet away, Legion came to an abrupt halt, a surprised look on his face and the tip of an arrow protruding from his chest. He reached up and felt it, as if he didn't believe it was there. While he was doing that, a second arrow punched through his body, just an inch from the first.

Neeley looked past Legion. A tall woman in a grey cloak, face hidden by a hood, held a short bow and was notching a third arrow.

Neeley drew the Naga blade with her good hand and slit Legion's throat. He collapsed to the roof.

"We must get away from here," the woman said, releasing the tension on the bow.

Legion's body crumpled inward, turning to dust.

"Who are you?" Neeley demanded.

The woman pulled back her hood. In the light reflecting up from the searchlights, she revealed short white hair and pale, unblemished skin, so smooth it appeared almost plastic. Neeley recognized her from the debriefs of Doc's mission: Thyia, daughter of Pyrrha, mythically the granddaughter of Pandora, but according to Doc's debrief she claimed they were 'sisters' from a timeline called Gaia which also fought the Shadow. Except for those of her planet who were rogue and fought for the Shadow.

"The one who just saved you. Come with me. There might be more."

"You're Thyia," Neeley said.

"You don't have the Sight," Thyia said. "How do you know that?"

"One of my team, Doc, met you."

Thyia nodded. "Yes. Twice. How does he fare?"

"He perished on a mission."

"The forever death?"

"Yes."

"Did he die honorably?"

"He sacrificed himself to save the rest of the team."

"There is no greater honor," Thyia said. "He was ill the last time we met. He wouldn't have lived much longer and would have suffered a painful, lingering ending. Better to go out quickly." She cocked her head. "Since you do not have the Sight . . ." She stood still for several moments.

Neeley used the opportunity to police up her pistol, which had not disappeared with the Legion.

Thyia finally spoke. "Do you know why you are here?"

"To keep history intact," Neeley said.

"Yes, yes," Thyia said, "but do you know what the Shadow has planned?"

"No."

Thyia sighed, disappointed. "Come." She walked away and didn't look over her shoulder to see if Neeley was following. They entered a stairwell and descended. To the terminal level and continued downward. Exiting the stairwell, they entered a tunnel where rusting tracks stretched in a long curve in either direction. The walls were damp and there was a foul odor.

"Where are we going?" Neeley asked as Thyia turned left.

"There's a disturbance," Thyia said. "I can feel where the Legion entered this time and place." She paused at a dented steel door. There were bullet marks in the concrete all around it. Red scorch marks in the limestone framed the opening. The download confirmed this was where the film had been stored and burned for days. Thyia squeezed in. There were blackened limestone walls. Whatever else had been in here had burned to ash, except for a row of Russian radio transmitters set on tables along one wall. The lines for their antennas snaked up through a hole drilled in the concrete roof.

"What's that?" Neeley asked.

"The Russians had a command post here at the end of the war," Thyia said. "It was abandoned when the city was divided."

But the gear is still here, Neeley thought. "Why are we here?" she asked as Thyia retrieved the bow from underneath her cloak and notched an arrow. She didn't draw the string, but focused on the center of the large chamber.

Neeley ripped a piece of cloth off the coat, not a difficult task given the poor condition of the material and tried to wrap it tight around her wrist with her good hand and using her teeth.

"You are injured?" Thyia asked.

Neeley fought the urge to channel her inner Scout and say: *Duh*. "Yes. Something's broken."

Thyia put her bow and notched arrow down. She tossed aside the makeshift bandage. Pulled a piece of white linen from inside her cloak. She felt Neeley's wrist. "Not serious. You can still use it if you can stand the pain."

"I can handle the pain," Neeley confirmed. Then fought back a gasp as Thyia wrapped the linen around the wrist tightly, cinching it down with jerk that seemed overly aggressive. But when she was done, while she didn't have movement, Neeley had a workable wrist.

Thyia picked up the bow once more.

"What's going on?" Neeley asked.

"Something is coming," Thyia said.

"What?"

"We'll see when it arrives. It's complicated and involves more than just here and now."

"Great," Neeley muttered. She made sure she had a round in the chamber of the forty-five.

AREA 51

There were a dozen old bullet holes in the rusting sign. The faded lettering read:

SEE ALL THE POISINUS SNAKES 75cents.

"I like that," Angus said, squeezed in the Humvee backseat between Ivar and Orlando. Jace was driving, one of his team members was in the passenger seat, and a third was manning the fifty-caliber machinegun in the center hatch. A second Humvee with the rest of the Nightstalkers was following.

Jace stopped and displayed his security badge at two guards who popped up out of hide holes, weapons ready. The Humvees were also painted with a laser designator and Hellfire missiles mounted on a nearby ridgeline were targeted on them and slaved to the triggers on the guard's weapons. If they fired, the missiles would come screaming in.

Just in case.

One of the guards retinal scanned Jace, then waved them through. Jace accelerated them down the dirt and sand trail toward a dilapidated barn whose doors appeared ready to fall off.

They were actually two-inch reinforced concrete and the least armored part of the barn.

"What are ye singing, lad?" Angus asked Ivar, who had not been aware he'd automatically gone into Barn mode.

"*Lawyers, Guns and Money*," Ivar said.

"Ah, Warren," Angus said. "I need to tell you 'bout the time I met him in Spain. He wrote *Roland the Headless Thompson Gunner* after a mate of mine from days gone by. Strange man."

Ivar wasn't sure whether he was referring to Warren Zevon or his mate and didn't ask.

The sensor above the Barn doors picked up the approach of the Humvee. Jace wasn't as talented as Eagle as he tapped the brakes to slow a bit as the large doors swung open. Eagle would have timed the approach just right, requiring no slowing.

The upgraded Snake was inside, ramp down. Similar to the tilt-rotor Osprey, this model had jet engines instead of rotors and numerous other modifications. It had a 30 millimeter chain gun mounted in the front under the cockpit. It fired uranium depleted core rounds and could take out a tank. There were Hellfire missiles ready for action on the wings.

As the second Humvee skidded to a halt, the barn doors closed. The Nightstalkers piled out and went into pre-mission prep, each member checking the gear that was their area of specialty. Angus, Orlando and Ivar stood to the side, staying out of the way.

Ivar noted that Jace had an acetated sheet that he was checking off as his team reported status. Ivar wondered if it were the same one Nada had used. Angus stirred as two of the Nightstalkers carried a large plastic container marked with a red skull and bones up the ramp. He joined them.

"What toys do ye have?"

One of the demo men flipped up the lid and let Angus explore. As he was doing this, Jace checked off the last item. The two engines came alive, their whine echoing off the reinforced walls of the Barn. The smell of burning jet fuel filled the air.

Angus began to pick items out of the demo box, placing them in a rucksack, much to the dismay of the Nightstalkers in charge of it as he disturbed the careful array of equipment.

"It don't do anyone any good sitting in there, lad," Angus assured him.

Jace went to one of the numerous dirty glass cases set on tables along one side of the shed. A sign warned *Danger: Extremely Poisinus*. Jace reached in and hit the open button. The ramp was coming up as he ran back and hopped on it.

Powerful hydraulic arms split the top of the Barn, pushing the halves apart and revealing the sky. The wings rotated to vertical.

Jace stood on the ramp, swaying as the aircraft lifted. Everyone else was seated on the red web benches along the outside of the aircraft. The pilot cleared the still opening roof with a few inches to spare on either wingtip.

They didn't have a long flight. Across Nevada 375 and to Area 51.

"We're going in circles," Angus muttered, the words lost in the sound of the engines. He cinched his seat belt. "Buckle up," he warned Ivar. "Gravity rules."

Orlando tapped him on the shoulder and leaned close, shouting to be heard. "Weapons?" He indicated a large box strapped to the cargo bay floor.

Angus displayed the Leatherman on his belt. "This will do until we know what we're facing."

Orlando looked at Ivar inquisitively. Ivar remembered how easily the Israeli commando took him down on the previous mission. Shooting wasn't what he was here for. He shook his head.

The Snake banked hard and headed directly for the large opening in the side of Groom Mountain. The evacuated personnel had kindly left the huge hanger doors open and the Snake swooped in.

They touched down and Jace was shouting as the ramp lowered, getting his personnel off as quickly as possible. He was irritated as Angus unbuckled and strolled down the ramp. As soon as they were all off, the Snake lifted, blowing sand and dust all around and exited the hanger, going into a stationery hover just outside, the 30mm chain gun pointed inside.

The Nightstalkers were tactically deployed inside the hanger, weapons at the ready.

Angus strolled across the concrete floor to the large freight elevator, Ivar and Orlando half a step behind. Angus turned and raised an eyebrow. Jace circled his hand over his head and the Nightstalkers joined.

"I'm going down to take a peep," Angus said. "Anyone like to join me?"

Jace indicated for two of his people to remain above. The rest joined Angus, Ivar and Orlando in the elevator. Angus shoved the lever and the elevator descended.

He wasn't humming the *The Girl From Ipanema.*

THE MISSION PHASE IV

NEW YORK CITY, 22 September 1776

"Why would General Howe let Rogers set you free?" Scout asked Hale.

"Major Rogers said he'd deal with the General. Convince him it was in his interest." Hale folded the papers, slid them back in the case and put it back inside his shirt, buttoning it up.

Scout had seen this type of fervent belief before and now it was reinforced with the possibility of escaping the noose. Who wouldn't believe a white figure floating in the air that spoke directly into your head?

"Rogers is lying," Scout said.

Hale frowned. "He has no reason to lie."

"Rogers hates Washington. I heard him speaking with General Howe. These papers are false. It's a trap for Washington."

"You lie."

"I have no reason to lie," Scout said.

"The angel certainly told the truth." He looked past her.

She glanced over her shoulder as the door opened and Major Rogers was framed in the entrance.

"You again," Rogers said. "As I said. We could make room for two on the gallows." He gestured to the squad of redcoats behind him. "Take him. It's time."

Two Redcoats grabbed Nathan Hale and directed him out of the greenhouse.

Rogers turned to Scout. "You're so curious? Come along, wench. Watch what happens to spies. We can share an ale afterward. And more."

A squad of soldiers was drawn up in front of the greenhouse, along with Captain Montressor on his horse. Hale was moved into the middle of the squad and Montressor gave the order to move out. They headed inland along a worn cart trail.

Scout followed behind the small contingent of Redcoats, who marched Hale along the dirt road to his fate. Rogers was near her, while Captain Montressor was in charge of the executing party. The captain rode at the head of the small column, stiff in the saddle, never looking over his shoulder at the condemned man. Scout followed, walking in the hazy dust the procession produced.

There was no gallows waiting for Nathan Hale. A noose dangled from a tree branch along the Post Road, at a spot that would one day become 66th Street and Third Avenue. A tavern was across the road from the execution site and spewed a crowd of onlookers as they arrived.

Scout wondered at the human desire to imbibe other's misery and death. As they came to the tree, Scout noted that a wagon was set off to the side, the bed empty, a barrel tied off on one side holding shovels, picks and axes. A man stood near the noose; the Provost Marshall, whose duty it was to ensure the sentence was carried out. General Howe was nowhere to be seen.

Montressor dismounted and conferred with the Provost.

Scout glanced at Major Rogers. He seemed pleased with himself and she wondered when he would produce the order from General Howe with the pardon?

Montressor and Hale went underneath a pavilion tent and spoke. Hale handed over the letters he'd written; one to his mother, the other to a fellow officer. That was correct according to the download. The patriot was composed, but he had reason to be. In fact, Montressor seemed more distressed at having to complete this task.

Finally, the time arrived. Nathan Hale was led to the cart, his hands bound behind him. It had been moved so the bed was beneath the rope. Two Redcoats pulled Hale onto it. The Provost awkwardly climbed up next to the condemned and read the charge with which the spy was accused.

Scout eyed the guards, who weren't particularly alert, given Hale's hands were tied. The crowd was morbidly curious, but not antagonistic. Those who were still in this area were mainly Loyalists who were content that law and order had been restored by the King's forces.

The Provost finished and turned to Hale. "Have you some words, sir?"

Hale nodded; chin thrust forward. "I do."

"Speak, sir."

Nathan Hale raised his voice to reach as far as possible. "I am so satisfied with the cause in which I have engaged, that my only regret is that I have not more lives than one to offer in its service."

The Provost waited for more, but there was none. He nodded and a sergeant slipped a black hood over Hale's head. Then the noose.

Scout looked at Major Rogers, expecting him to step forward with the pardon from General Howe.

The Provost, the guards, and the sergeant climbed off the wagon.

Scout sensed Rogers was enjoying playing God, cutting it close.

The executioner climbed into the front of the wagon and picked up the reins to the two horses.

"May God have mercy on your soul," the Provost called out. Then he nodded at the executioner.

The driver raised the reins and snapped them. The horses jolted forward.

As the wagon moved under his feet, Nathan Hale finally called out. "Major Rog—" the last of the name was cut off as his feet slid off the wagon and he dropped to the end of the rope.

His legs churned as he tried to run from inevitable death.

SALEM, MASSACHUSETTS. 22 September 1692

Lara knelt, using the haft of the Naga to keep from collapsing, breathing hard.

"Took you long enough," a familiar voice called down to her.

Standing on top of the boulder, above Unity, was Pandora. She was also breathing hard, sweat on her forehead.

"Did you—" Lara managed to get out.

"The girl initiated it," Pandora said. "I just gave her some additional strength." She jumped off the boulder, landing lightly between Lara and Unity Hale. "You don't think she did it all by herself, do you? She has the Sight, I'll grant you, but it's raw and unpolished. As you were once."

"Who are you?" Unity asked.

"Friends," Pandora replied.

"Who were they?" Unity was confused. "Where did they go?" She edged out of the crack in the boulder.

Lara got to her feet. She was drained of energy. Those three hadn't been Legion, the normal Shadow mercenary. They'd been her genetic brothers. She'd felt their deaths but had ignored the emotional impact at the instant each happened, but the cumulative effect had her confused and overwhelmed with a sense of despair.

Unity Hale came to her and placed a hand on Lara's chest, over her heart.

"You're in pain," Unity said. "Let me help."

And the fist that clenched Lara's heart loosened its grip and the tightness around her chest was gone and she could breath. "Thank you." She looked past Unity. "And thank you."

Pandora nodded in acknowledgement.

Unity Hale drew her hand back. She was tiny, barely five feet and perhaps seventy pounds. She had not yet entered her womanhood but emanated a palpable aura that Lara was sure even those without the Sight could sense. It would be why she would end up on Hallows Eve tied spread-eagle on the ground near the gallows, a board on her chest, with rocks piled on top, designed to slowly kill her, the *peine forte et dure*, a classic method of torture. Accused of being a witch.

"Who are you?" Unity asked once more.

"We're friends," Lara said, echoing Pandora and having a moment of empathy for Pandora's evasiveness.

"Who were they?" Unity repeated, waving her hand to indicate the now gone Lukas.

"Not friends," was the best Lara could come up with, which earned her an eye roll from Pandora, which Lara thought a smidge hypocritical.

"What are you doing out here alone at night, young girl?" Pandora asked.

What are you, her mother? Lara thought, but it was the same question she'd been about to ask, so she refrained.

"Thinking," Unity said. "But you have not told me who you are or who those men were. Where did they go?"

"It shouldn't concern you now," Pandora said.

"I believe they meant me harm," Unity Hale disagreed. "They

were unlike any I have ever met before. They were—" she couldn't find the words.

"Gray shadows," Lara said.

"Yes!" Unity said.

"Do you sense that in me?" Lara asked.

Unity stared at her. "No." The young girl smiled sadly. "You're struggling like I am. But you don't mean me, or anyone else, harm. You want to help."

Lara looked at Pandora as if to say: *See!*

"You must get back to the village," Pandora chided Unity. "It isn't safe to be out here in the dark. You're lucky my friend and I came along or those highwaymen might have hurt you."

"'Highwaymen'?" Unity repeated. "What does that mean?"

"Thieves," Lara simplified.

It didn't help Unity much. "But where did they go? I don't understand."

Lara picked up an abrupt change in Pandora. "What's wrong?"

Unity felt it also. "Someone is hurt."

"Thyia," Pandora said. "My sister."

"Where is she?" Unity said. "We can help."

"No," Pandora said. "We can't. Not from here." She faced Unity. "You need to go home, girl."

Unity disagreed. "Morning will be soon enough to return to Salem. For that is when they will try to hang eight more good souls."

"It's a terrible thing," Lara agreed. "But it's not something that—"

"I am going to stop it," Unity said with not just the certainty of naïve youth, but with a strength both Pandora and Lara could feel.

"How?" Lara asked.

"I can make people feel certain ways," Unity said. "I've always had this ability."

"You edge them," Lara said.

Unity cocked her head, her smooth forehead wrinkled with a frown and then she nodded. "Yes. That's a good term for it. I can push them into doing something without them knowing I'm helping."

Pandora cut in. "This isn't about getting an extra cookie from your mother, young girl. This is life and death."

Unity turned to face the older woman, faux Goddess. "My mother died bringing me forth into the world. And now I will be joining her."

"What?" Lara exclaimed.

Unity said it as if it were no large matter: "I am going to convince the people to hang me instead of the eight condemned. And they will do it, because I will make them do it and I will save eight innocent lives."

WASHINGTON D.C.. 22 September 1862

"Mister President," Eagle said. "There is no dilemma. You have the Proclamation. It supersedes the Declaration and negates any offer from the Confederacy."

Lincoln gave a sad smile. "You should know, or perhaps you do already, that the twist to the Emancipation Proclamation is that it only frees the slaves in territory of the Confederacy. In effect in land we have no control over. At its core, it is a gesture with little teeth."

"That is true," the Keep urged. "A delay would be wise."

"It is symbolic as a promise for the future," Eagle said, speaking quickly. He had one hand in his pocket, fingering the item that Edith had given him right after the mission briefing. "It will give hope to the three and a half million of my brothers and sisters who bear the yoke of slavery." But echoing in his own mind, he thought of how many more would die in this war. How the brief shining light of Reconstruction would essentially be over after Grant's second term as President and then a century of Jim Crow, which was as close as to slavery as one could get without calling it that. Could there be a better way? Was the Keep correct? The war would go on regardless.

Eagle shook that off. *Stick to the mission.*

Lincoln laid his head back against the chair and closed his eyes. "It is wearisome bearing these burdens." He lifted a finger, indicating the desk. "The papers are full of the casualty rolls from Antietam. I am trying to make it appear a success today. But McClellan refused to go after Lee. He says he is concerned for his troops. A bit late for that it appears to me. He constantly complains he is outnumbered. Even I, no military strategist, sitting here in Washington, know that cannot be true. He is fearful of Lee. Seward asked me to delay the Proclamation until there was a victory or else it might seem an act of desperation to keep Europe at bay. He said it would be a 'last shriek of retreat' but Seward is apt to exaggerate at times."

"Perhaps some tea, Mister President?" the Keep asked, indicating the kettle on a small stove in the corner of the room, next to a low cupboard.

Lincoln nodded. "That would suit the mood."

The Keep rolled herself to the stove and prepared three cups.

Eagle accessed the download. "Mister President. You have not touched the 'institution' as you call it since the start of the war; which is being fought over that very 'institution'. By simply announcing the existence of the Emancipation Proclamation today, you are giving fair notice of your ultimate purpose, to all the States and to all the people. This gives all the option to turn aside from the institution. For the rebelling states and people to once again become good citizens of the United States. It will be their choice if they chose to disregard it."

Lincoln's eyes narrowed. "Fine words. As if I said them myself."

"Could you help?" the Keep asked, holding up a shaking hand,

and indicating the kettle. "I fear pouring hot water on myself. I've prepared the cups."

Eagle went over and poured, keeping his focus on the President. He took one over to Lincoln.

"No choice is clear-cut," Lincoln said. "Compromise is the essence of effective governing. Note, I say effective. Not necessarily good or right. I have to send secret missives to my commander in the west, General Grant, to allow southern black-market traders to pass with their contraband through our lines on the Mississippi. Cotton. The very material which makes owning other human beings lucrative, thus I am indirectly allowing something grievous. But we need the cotton, you see? Or else how could we make the uniforms for our young men who are giving their lives to end that very practice? Does any of that make sense? Is it two-faced of me?" Lincoln shook his head. "I am tired of the constant battling. I will delay the announcement."

"Sir—" Eagle began, but Lincoln's patience was worn through.

"Enough!"

Eagle pulled the item out of his pocket and held it out, remaining silent.

Lincoln had the tea in one hand. He reached out with the other. He examined the penny in the light from the window. "What is this?"

"A one cent piece, sir," Eagle said.

"It is not," Lincoln said. "Is this some sort of joke? Why is my visage on this? Some sort of ceremonial thing?"

"It is what my people use, sir," Eagle said.

Lincoln was examining it more closely. "What is this number next to my profile?"

"The date, sir."

Lincoln looked up sharply. "It cannot be."

"It is, sir," Eagle said.

"But it says twenty-twenty."

. . .

MANCHESTER, NEW YORK. 22 September 1823

Roland lost track of how many timelines they visited even though he tried. His best estimate was sixteen, but it had been hard because sometimes he swapped out one plate, other times two, several times three and even none once. It was kinda confusing keeping tabs on all the numbers. Occasionally, they were met by people who spoke something close to English or even the same language.

Once there was no one there, just the sarcophagus with the plates. Roland had removed the top and done as Lachesis instructed. Another time there'd been no sarcophagus or people. They'd waited an anxious couple of minutes, then Lachesis had opened a Gate and they'd moved on.

He knew the debrief was going to be a nightmare as he would have to recall all he'd seen. He also knew someone, probably Ivar, was going to make fun of his ability to count. And that Neeley would give him a comforting hand to keep him from getting upset.

If everyone made it back.

They came out on a hillside that for a moment he thought was his own timeline, but quickly realized wasn't as a half-dozen women surrounded them. They were dressed in grey cloaks and held short bows, arrows notched, strings drawn.

There was no sign of a sarcophagus. A woman strode through, taller than the rest. She pulled back her hood to reveal dark hair with a silver streak in it.

"Is that Pandora?" Roland asked Lachesis. She matched the description, albeit younger.

"Hush," Lachesis said.

"How do you know me?" Pandora demanded of Roland.

"Not the one your team has met," Lachesis responded to Roland in a low voice. She spoke louder. "Where are the plates?"

"Close by, wise one," Pandora said. "Who is he? Why do you bring a man?"

"He's helping me," Lachesis responded.

Pandora snorted in contempt. "Manual labor is all they are good for."

"They are useful for more than that," Lachesis said. "Or else you would not exist. Bring the plates."

"We require something in exchange, wise one," Pandora said.

"What?"

"Knowledge, oh wise one. After all, the plates contain wisdom we have not been able to decipher yet. And we bring them freely. So you are taking something from us, are you not?"

"It is not freely," Lachesis noted, "if you desire something in return."

"You are correct," Pandora said. "We offer it freely." She raised a hand and four women came forward from the forest carrying the sarcophagus. "But we would appreciate any wisdom you could impart."

"You 'offer'?" Lachesis sniffed.

The four women removed the stone top. Lachesis went to it, going through the same routine. She ordered Roland to replace two plates. "See? I do not take without giving," Lachesis said.

Pandora indicated the tablets. "We have made sense of some of the markings. Some touches on the legend of the One. Can you tell us more about this so we can fight the Shadow?"

"No," Lachesis said. "Come," she said to Roland and they stepped into a Gate.

As they traversed the tunnel, Lachesis said: "You see? You're not the only one I don't explain things too."

He knew Lachesis was done when they stepped out of the Gate and there was Joseph Smith, hands still raised in supplication to the Valkyrie.

"First plate here," Lachesis told him, indicating a slot. "Next. And finally."

Roland was glad to be done hauling the gold plates. He was in good shape, excellent shape actually, but had been getting a bit worn down manhandling them. "What now?" he asked as the last plate slid into place.

"Now things are set aright," Lachesis said. "As aright as possible given circumstances."

"What things?" Roland wanted to know. "What are these plates?"

"You wouldn't understand even if I explained it," Lachesis said.

"Try," Roland said. "Pandora said something about the One."

"She was, what is the term? Fishing."

Roland indicated the sarcophagus. "That's it? That's my mission? Hauling stuff around for you?"

Lachesis faced him. "I told you it was. And it does not stand alone among your team's missions."

"What does that mean?" Roland shook his head. "How are these plates connected?"

"Have you ever successfully done a Rubik's cube?" Lachesis asked.

"That colored plastic thing?"

"Yes."

"No."

"I can't explain it to you then."

"I saw Doc do it a couple of times," Roland said. "I bet Ivar could. And if you explain to me, I can explain it to him."

"It was a metaphor," Lachesis said. "Put the lid back on, please."

"I know what a metaphor is," Roland grumbled as he replaced the heavy stone on top. He stepped back and faced the Fate. "What now?"

"I am done."

"Why am I still here if this was my mission?" Roland asked.

"Because I enjoy conversing with you," Lachesis said.

Roland frowned, trying to determine if there was a tone of sarcasm in that statement.

She crooked a finger and Roland followed her out of the clearing and into the trees, a distance from the plates, Smith and the Valkyries.

Roland felt a shiver as time resumed and a breeze blew through the trees.

"How do you do that?" Roland asked. "Stop time."

"I didn't stop time," Lachesis said.

"We were in a fold of time?" Roland asked.

Lachesis raised a white eyebrow. "A very good metaphor."

"I *am* done here?" Roland asked.

"Are you anxious to return—" Lachesis paused. "Ah! You're concerned for someone. Someone that you love."

"I'm worried about my team," Roland admitted.

"But your love is for one specific person," Lachesis said.

Roland bristled. "I told you to stay out of my head."

"I'm not in your head," Lachesis said. "I've been around a long time. I can read people."

Roland took a step toward her, but she raised her hand and he halted.

"Now I am in your head," Lachesis said. "Her name is Neeley and she went to Berlin. 1947." She closed her eyes. "Oh dear. That will not do at all. It seems our work is not quite done." The Fate's eyes opened and she lifted her rod. "Love is a powerful thing that sometimes transcends space and time. She will need your help."

And with a wave of Fate's rod, Roland was in the tunnel of time.

AREA 51. 22 September 1947

The Shadow has already changed things, Moms thought. Between the gold plate and Fat Man, neither of which were reported as being in here according to the download, things were different. She was too late.

"Are you all right?" Jordan asked. "Do you need some water? I know, seeing an A-Bomb is a shock, especially with a guy like Thorn having his hand on the trigger. I don't know what he's afraid of, but then again, none of us know what to expect when we activate the Arch."

"They took bets on Trinity," Moms muttered.

"Excuse me?" Jordan said, not quite hearing her.

"They took bets on Trinity's yield. Some wagered it would wipe out the world, which makes you wonder what they expected to collect."

"Oh. Physicists. We're an odd bunch," Jordan said. "I worked at Oak Ridge. Missed all the excitement at Los Alamos. We heard about everything when the general public did. We didn't even know about the Gadget and Trinity until after they detonated. They had good security."

Moms wondered if that was it. Good security? Is that why there was no record of a gold plate and Fat Man down here? Or had history already changed? Could she change it back?

"What do you think will happen?" Jordan asked.

"I've got no idea," Moms lied.

Jordan laughed. "You're probably the only honest person down here. Everyone's got an opinion. But really? This is way beyond the bomb. There, we understood the physics. Here, we're kids playing with . . ." he trailed off.

"Something you don't understand," Moms finished for him.

"Yes," Jordan said.

"Where did the gold plate come from?" Moms asked.

"I don't know," Jordan said. "It was here the first time I came down. There's a bunch of rumors about it, but no one seems to know for certain. Most agree it was recovered during the war."

"From where?"

Jordan shrugged. "Your guess us as good as anybody's." He lowered his voice. "To be honest, I'm not happy about the company. My older brother was killed off of Okinawa. Kamikaze. I don't hold an entire people responsible, but these particular people, these so-called scientists." He shook his head. "I didn't know I'd getting involved with people like that when I signed up for the Manhattan Project."

"We were at war then," Moms noted. "This isn't the Manhattan Project any more."

"True." Jordan checked his watch as the level of activity around the Arch increased. "Five minutes."

The hair on the back of her neck rose, a sensation Moms was familiar with. "A Rift is forming."

"A what?"

Moms had a forty-five inside her jacket. Not good enough by far. She missed Roland and his machinegun and flamer, but there was a good chance Roland was dead, given the gold plate.

"A Rift," Moms said.

"Whoa!" Jordan said. "Look!"

The symbols on the gold plate were changing, morphing into something different and the calculations were shifting.

"Roland," Moms whispered.

"What?" Jordan asked.

There was no time for this. Moms spotted Colonel Thorn standing near Fat Man and strode to him, Jordan trailing her, confused.

A long wire stretched from Fat Man to a red button secured under a locked panel on the wall. Thorn was in front of it. Moms noted he had a key in hand.

"Colonel," Moms said.

The soldier's eyes were on the Arch and scientists. "Yes?"

"A Rift is going to open in that Arch," Moms said. "Bad things called Fireflies are going to come through."

"Define Rift," Thorn said, unperturbed. He checked his watch. "We got four minutes, so make it snappy."

"We don't know for certain," Moms said. "It's either a crack in space or time or both. To a parallel world."

That earned her a sideways glance of the sunglasses. Jordan was listening, but not intervening.

"Things are going to come through," Moms continued. "They look like little gold sparkles. We need to account for every one of them. They go into things." She swept her hand indicating the work area. "Not humans. Any object, any creature. Takes it over. A Firefly can animate an object, turn it into a weapon."

She had Thorn's full attention. "How do you know this? Why should I believe you?"

"You'll learn I'm right shortly. If I'm wrong, I'm wrong. You need more men down here."

Thorn didn't hesitate. "Sergeant!" he called out.

One of the guards at the elevator snapped to attention. "Get the reaction force here and scramble everyone. Now!"

"Sir!"

The sergeant snatched the phone and began issuing orders.

"How do we kill these things?" Thorn asked, in the vein of Roland.

"Blast whatever there're inside of into pieces, then flame it."

"Flamethrowers," Thorn yelled to the Sergeant who was still speaking into the phone. The enlisted man gave a thumbs up to indicate he understood.

"When the Firefly is done it comes out of the object and dissipates," Moms said.

Jordan spoke up. "How do you know this? How do you know it will create a tear in space-time?"

"Do *you* know what it's gonna do?" Moms shot back.

Jordan had no reply.

"You won't need that," Moms added, indicating Fat Man.

"You got a crystal ball?" Thorn asked. "These damn scientists. Always messing with things they don't understand or control. Couple of them told me they were afraid Trinity would cause a chain reaction and ignite the atmosphere and destroy the world. I'm not taking any chances with this thing." He indicated the Arch. Nevertheless. he stuck the key in a pocket and drew his forty-five.

Moms took that as approval and drew her own.

Thorn smiled grimly. "I like a woman who comes prepared to dance." He checked the time. "One minute."

The freight elevator opened and a platoon of soldiers exited. They were armed with M-1s and Thompson submachineguns. Four had flamethrowers. They spread out around the cavern.

A man in a white coat walked up to Thorn. He had a strong German accent. "What is this?"

"I was a Boy Scout," Thorn said. "Being prepared."

Further discussion was negated as the air crackled with static electricity. A black, vertical line appeared in the center of the Arch. It widened; a shimmering darkness that filled the space surrounded by the metal.

The Fireflies came through, too many and too fast to count. One flew straight into a test engine and a second later it ignited. The flame roared twenty feet, incinerating several scientists who were frozen in surprise at what was happening.

Thorn's men might have been surprised but they reacted immediately. They opened up on the engine, bullets striking metal. Another Firefly went into a fire hose, something Moms had seen before. She fired the forty-five at the hose as it came alive, whipping out and wrapping around a soldier's neck, breaking it. She was trying to sever it, shorten the length the Firefly had to work with, but it was moving fast.

Most of the Fireflies chose the nearest thing to take over: the numerous cables going into the Arch, tearing them off and whipping them through the air. There was a method behind it as soldiers were killed, but the men in white coats were pulled into the Rift. She saw Jordan being pulled toward the Arch but the Firefly, not being subtle or particularly aware, slammed his head against the metal as he went and blood and brains splattered, then the body was gone into the Rift.

The jet engine crashed to the floor, no longer functional.

"Flame it!" Moms yelled at one of the flame throwers.

He torched what remained and a golden spark floated out of the debris, then dissipated.

Moms grabbed a Thompson lying next to a dead soldier. She tucked it tight to her shoulder and fired short bursts,, finally severing the hose, leaving a writhing segment about five feet long.

"Flame!" She screamed.

At that moment, though, a Firefly went into one of the flamethrowers, taking control. The barrel turned toward the man who had it strapped on his back, despite his desperate efforts to stop it. It flared and the man screamed briefly before Moms fired, killing him. She emptied the magazine into the flamethrower and it exploded, sending shrapnel flying. The Firefly floated up and dissipated.

Moms felt a tug of pain on her side, but grabbed a full magazine off the body of a soldier, slamming it home. Colonel Thorn was next to her, both firing controlled bursts.

There was so much going on that Moms almost missed the most critical element. Fat Man was slowly rolling toward the Rift under the arch. Moms paused in shooting to understand what she was seeing, then realized a Firefly had gotten into the metal cradle the bomb rested on. The wheels were trundling the ten thousand, three-hundred-pound bomb across the floor, animated by the presence of a Firefly.

"Colonel," Moms shouted, getting Thorn's attention. She gestured.

Together they fired at one of the metal wheels of the cradle. Their rounds ricocheted off, careening across the cavern. The noise in the cavern was deafening at Thorn's soldiers were shooting at different targets, but the objects that were possessed by Fireflies were pulling back, coalescing around Fat Man. Four heavy power cords controlled by Fireflies were wrapped around the bomb, helping to pull it toward the Rift.

Moms looked; the Demon Core was gone, already sucked in.

"Damn it!" Thorn exclaimed. He pulled the key out of his pocket.

"What are you doing?" Moms demanded, but Thorn ignored her.

He stuck the key in the covering, unlocked and flipped it up. He didn't hesitate, slamming his fist on the red button.

Nothing happened.

Moms was frozen for a moment, but as Thorn ran for Fat Man and she followed. They both leapt on top of the bomb as it passed into the Rift.

BERLIN, 22 September 1948

"Why are you helping?" Neeley asked.

"The enemy of your enemy, is your enemy's enemy," Thyia said.

"That's what you told Doc," Neeley said. "Kind of off from the way we say it."

"You have not battled the Shadow as long as we have," Thyia said. "Your team mate Doc asked if we were friends because we both fought the Shadow. One cannot have friends across time-lines. Because, in the end, it will always be about where we come from."

"The Shadow must like that attitude," Neeley said. "Yet, you saved my life. You saved Doc. You're here waiting for whatever is going to show up. Why?"

Thyia glanced at her. "Sometimes missions cross timelines. Whatever could happen here has the potential to destroy your timeline."

"But you don't know what that is and it hasn't happened yet," Neeley pointed out. "If your Sight warned you of that, how come our people with Sight haven't picked up the same?"

Thyia sighed. "We received a message from the Ones Before."

"Telling you what?"

"To be here. To help."

"That's it?" Neeley pressed.

"That's it."

"Bullshit," Neeley said. "You just told me your timeline, Gaia, doesn't believe in making friends with other timelines. You have a vested interest, obviously, in ours. That's because of the One, correct? You thought Alexander the Great was the One, but you were wrong. You have no idea who it is, but for some reason, you believe this person comes from our timeline, right? The One who will defeat the Shadow?"

Thyia was quiet for a little bit, then said: "That is the prophecy."

"Why this timeline?" Neeley asked.

"No one knows."

"Who made the prophecy?"

"I am not here to be interrogated by you," Thyia said. "You are —" she paused and closed her eyes. "It's opening."

The Gate snapped into existence; a darkness deeper than the absence of light. Six feet high, by four wide. Even so, the creature that came through had to duck. It was seven feet tall and covered in white fur that gleamed in the few flickering lights in the room. A bigger, more dangerous grizzly would be understating the Yeti.

It growled as it straightened, revealing long fangs. It spread muscled arms wide, razor sharp claws ready to grab and tear.

Thyia pulled drew the string on her bow and let loose within two seconds of it appearing. Neeley was a fraction behind, firing the forty-five as fast as she could pull the trigger, sending the large slugs into center of the creature's face. Thousands of hours of range time paid off as all eight rounds struck home. The Yeti was so large the impact of the bullets didn't knock it back, but they did shatter bone and teeth. One round went through the roof of mouth and penetrated into the brain.

The beast was not happy with that as it howled in pain and rage. It staggered forward toward them.

Thyia let loose another arrow as Neeley dropped the magazine and slammed another home.

"The eyes," Thyia yelled as her third arrow ricocheted off the ridge of bone just above the Yeti's left eye. Both women were giving ground, backing up toward the vault door. The problem was one would have to turn their back to open it.

Neeley did as Thyia suggested and her third round of the second magazine struck home, plowing into a beady red eyeball, through it and into the brain. This served to antagonize the beast even more. It seemed two working eyes and a complete brain were not essential to its mission of destruction.

Thyia threw aside the bow as the Yeti came within reach and she leapt at it, Naga dagger in hand. Neeley expended the last of her bullets and drew her dagger. Yeti embraced Thyia's attack, wrapping long arms around her and sinking the claws into her back. She stabbed at the other eye, finally sinking the blade in and completely blinding the beast.

Neeley took the opening and dashed behind the Yeti. She sliced through the tendons at the base of its ankles and the legs gave way, the knees buckling. There was a palpable shiver in the room as it slammed to the floor and then over. Thyia jerked the blade out of the eye and jammed it deep into the throat then pulled it sideways with her remaining strength.

She was rewarded with a spray of gray blood drenching her.

Neeley went to Thyia, uncertain how to help her, given the claws impaled in her back, but that was solved at the Yeti disintegrated into dust. Thyia dropped to the pitted concrete flaw, blood flowing from eight, deep wounds.

Neeley was surprised none had been immediately fatal. "You'll be fine," she lied as she put pressure with each hand on two of the wounds, but it was impossible to tell which of them was the worst.

Thyia turned her head. She managed to gasp: "I must go. Step back. I fear something else is coming."

Neeley let go and moved away as a gate outlined Thyia on the floor and then she was gone.

Leaving Neeley alone with bloody hands in the scorched room deep under Tempelhof to await 'something else'.

The hair on the back her neck tingled.

A Rift was forming.

AREA 51

The elevator rumbled to a halt. The accompanying Nightstalkers had their weapons at the ready as the freight doors opened.

"Not good," Angus said as a wave of static washed over them. He indicated for everyone to remain on the elevator. Except for Ivar. He crooked his finger. "Come on."

"Great," Ivar muttered.

They walked into the large cavern that had once housed Odessa and was now part of the Area 51 Archives. The space was full of crates and machinery and quite a few objects that weren't readily identifiable as to their purpose.

Ivar did recognize some from Nightstalkers missions. Experiments and machinery recovered from scientists who'd screwed up. Minus the scientists, of course, since most screw-ups involved a fatal mistake.

"What are we feeling?" Angus asked as he led the way along an aisle between stacked crates.

"It feels like . . ." Ivar trailed off, because he knew exactly what it was.

"What, lad?" Angus asked as they reached an intersection. The old man looked over his shoulder. The Nightstalkers were fifty feet away, still in the elevator, weapons at the ready.

"A Rift," Ivar said.

"Where?" Angus asked.

"Close."

"Close as in hand grenades or double-tap or tactical nuclear weapon blast range?" Angus asked.

"I don't know," Ivar said. He slowly turned in a circle, then pointed along the open way to the left. "Down there."

"How come we're not being attacked by those Firefly thingies?" Angus asked.

"I don't know."

"Jesus, Mary and Joseph, lad, I brought you along for what you do know." Angus strode off in the directed indicated.

Ivar was reluctant to follow, because the Rift was doing strange things to his head. Voices of other Ivar's echoed in his brain. He wasn't sure if they were real or imagined, but what did it matter? They were there arguing with each other at a level just below being understood.

Ivar shuffled after Angus.

The old man held up a fist, indicating a halt. "Did you see that?"

"What?"

Angus shook his head, uncertain for the first time. "Looked like an old lady dressed in white standing down there. But she's gone. Strange things." He turned to the right and pointed at something large covered with a tarp. He indicated for Ivar to grab the other end of the tarp as he took the left bottom side.

Ivar wanted to protest, to say this wasn't a good idea, but the voices in his head left him speechless. He grabbed the trap.

Together they pulled and cloth fell away, revealing a shiny

steel arch, twenty feet high. The area under was filled with a shimmering gold Rift.

The surface was flickering and Angus cocked his head. "You see that, lad?"

Ivar tried to quiet the voices in his head and focus. There *was* something appearing in flashes.

A voice called out to their right, startling Ivar and irritating Angus.

"Clear?" Jace yelled, leaning around the corner.

Angus simply a hand up, indicating not to be disturbed. "There!"

A brief flicker and Neeley was standing alone in a dimly lit chamber, the walls scorched. She was splattered with blood. She held the forty-five in her hand, which had a bandaged wrist.

Then she was gone, the golden shimmer back.

"I saw it!" Ivar said.

"The lass is in trouble," Angus said. He indicated the Arch. "Can we go through?"

Ivar swallowed hard. "I have. But . . ."

"But what, lad?" When Ivar didn't answer, he snapped. "Can I go through or not?"

"I guess."

"Guesses get one killed," Angus said, but he took a step forward, just inches from the gold shimmer. "Ever see that movie, Butch Cassidy and Sundance?" he asked.

"What?"

"Remember when they jumped into the river together?" Angus held out a callused hand. "We're only gonna get a quick window, lad."

Ivar stood shoulder to shoulder with Angus and gripped his hand.

Neeley appeared in the Arch.

Angus stepped forward with Ivar at his side.

THE MISSION PHASE V

NEW YORK CITY, 22 September 1776

Scout blinked, not quite sure she was seeing what was playing out, so convinced she had been that Rogers had gotten Howe to agree to his plan. Why make up the maps? The plans?

Hale's legs slowed, then stopped moving after an agonizingly long forty seconds. A hard dying.

The crowd was silent and then began to drift away, the anticipation of the event dissipating with the reality of death. Most went into the tavern to wash away the morbid with alcohol and relish their own living.

Rogers finally moved, pushing forward to the wagon. He hopped up next to the driver. "Back up," he ordered.

"Hey there!" Captain Montressor shouted. "What are you doing, Rogers?"

The Ranger pulled a piece of parchment out of the inside pocket of his green fringed coat. "Order from General Howe. I'm to take the body to Rebel lines so that it might get a decent burial." As Montressor perused the document, Rogers climbed over into the bed. He ripped off the hood. Hale's face was contorted, his tongue extended, mouth agape, face bright red, eyes lifeless.

"Have some respect, man," Montressor said. "He died bravely. That's more than many a man can say."

"He's dead regardless," Rogers replied. He pointed to the executioner still sitting on the bench. "Give me a hand here or I'll be cutting your fine rope."

The executioner climbed back and Rogers lifted the body while the man extracted the rope from Hale's neck with great difficulty and then removed it.

Rogers unceremoniously let go of the freed body and it thumped into the bed of the wagon. "I'll be off, then."

"At least cover the man," Montressor protested.

Rogers waited impatiently as the Captain grabbed a cloak. Montressor cut the bonds on Hale's wrists and comported the body, legs together, arms crossed on the chest. He placed the cloak over Hale's face and upper body. As Montressor went to jump down, Rogers snapped the reins and the horses started forward, almost causing the Captain to fall.

"Damn you, Rogers!" Montressor cursed as the Ranger commander drove north.

"Frak me," Scout whispered to herself, realizing the genius of Rogers' plan. A dead man was much more convincing than a live one. Once Rogers turned the body over, as an apparent gesture of chivalry, it would be searched and the hidden plans discovered.

Edith's download, ever ready, intruded with some historical information, that had nothing to do with Hale, but was part of the overall military strategy portion: Operation Mincemeat. During World War II, the British had taken the corpse of a homeless man, dressed him up as an officer in the Royal Marines and planted papers and maps on him indicating the allies were preparing to invade Greece, rather than Sicily. They'd dumped the body at sea off the coast of supposedly neutral Spain. When the Spanish recovered the body, they turned the information over to the German embassy which forwarded it to German intelligence and the diversion was effective because the corpse was believed to be that which it appeared. In this case, Hale *was* what he was: a spy sent personally by General Washington to find out exactly that which was secreted on his body.

Except Rogers had come up with the ploy one hundred and seventy years before the British secret service.

Scout accessed the download for information on what had happened to Nathan Hale's body. And drew a big blank. It disappeared with no indication of final resting place. It most definitely was not turned over to the Colonists, nor was there any record of what the British did with it.

Lost to history, which seemed a bit odd.

Scout remained by the tree as Montressor marched the Redcoats away. Rogers, and the wagon, disappeared over a rise in the dirt road heading in the opposite direction.

Then Scout set out to the north at a steady run. As she came over the rise, Rogers was waiting for her, pistol at the ready, standing behind the wagon.

"I know there be something off about you, lass." He nodded at the body behind him. "Were you some beau of his? Why do you care so much? Or are you a spy like him?"

Scout walked toward Rogers. "Does the famous Major Rogers, leader of the Rangers, need a pistol to capture a mere girl? I'm a Christian. I wish to make sure the body gets a decent burial."

Rogers laughed, un-cocked the pistol and tucked it back into the broad leather belt. "Perhaps we can make a deal, girl. I'll take you with me to the rebel's lines. But first, you have to—"

He didn't finish as Scout moved, quicker than a human was normally capable of doing. However, she was anything but a normal human. She snatched the pistol out of his belt before he could react and backed off, out of reach, cocking the gun.

"What was that?" Rogers shook his head. "How could you move so fast? Are you a witch? A demon? I was never a religious man, but after what I've seen this morning, I've been re-evaluating that. Who are you? What are you?"

"I'm justice," Scout said. She looked about. A cart trail cut off to the right into a copse of trees. "Get in the driver's seat."

As Rogers climbed up front and sat on the bench, Scout hopped up in the bed of the wagon, next to the body. "Move. On that trail to the right."

Rogers snapped the reins, trying to knock Scout out of the back, but she'd anticipated that. "I'm tempted to kill you," she said as they left the main north-south track and disappeared into the trees.

"What are you, girl?" Rogers asked as they rolled along a leaf-arched tunnel.

"I told you. Justice." A small clearing was to the left. "Stop there. Get out." Scout hopped off, pistol in hand, but not aimed.

Rogers reluctantly dismounted. "Are you going to shoot me in cold blood?"

"My blood is always warm," Scout said. "I don't need the gun." She swung it against the iron-rim around the wheel and the firing mechanism shattered.

Rogers, as she anticipated, took that as his signal to attack. He whipped out a knife from the back of his belt and came at her. But she had already moved and was behind him. She kicked him in the back his knee, sending him sprawling.

Rogers rolled and got to his feet, face redder than normal. He came at her, slashing, feinting, but never getting close.

"Save your energy," Scout advised. "You're going to need it." She glanced up. It was mid-afternoon so her bubble still had plenty of time if needed.

Rogers jabbed toward her gut, not even close, and then swung his arm up for a downward strike. Scout didn't move out of the way. She caught his forearm in an X formed by her arms and flowed, twisting, using his momentum. Rogers hit the ground so hard he lost the knife as the wind was knocked out of him. Scout picked up the knife and threw it into the forest.

Rogers rolled over, but didn't get up. His green coat was dirt-smeared and sweat trickled down his face. "You're no girl."

Scout pointed at the barrel of tools. "Get a shovel."

"Why should I?"

"You're going to bury Mister Hale."

"Washington's men will bury him. I was bringing him home."

"You were bringing him to Washington with false plans." Scout hopped up in the bed and unbuttoned Hale's shirt. She withdrew the oilskin. His skin was already cool and she shivered from the contact, thinking how he was alive not long ago and now there was nothing. The fagility of life so easily snuffed out.

"How'd you know about that?" Rogers demanded as he got to his feet. "You were skulking outside the General's office this morning, weren't you? I thought I heard someone."

Scout opened the pack and withdrew the papers. She tore them into small pieces. "Start digging his grave. Now."

"Still haven't given me a reason why—"

He didn't finish the sentence as Scout had her Naga blade out and slashed, cutting through his coat and shirt and leaving a thin line of red on his chest. "I can keep bleeding you until there's nothing left but a little stub of nothing."

For the first time, there was fear in Rogers' eyes. He pulled a shovel out of the barrel.

"There." Scout indicated a spot in the center of the clearing. As good a resting place as any. She wondered what would be standing here in her day. An apartment building? A skyscraper? A Starbucks? Would the bones be gone by then or just lost amidst the heavy machinery as the land was claimed?

As Rogers dug, Scout moved to the side and stood in the shade.

Rogers was mud-streaked when he finally climbed out of the hole. "This is deep enough to keep the animals from getting to him."

"Lay the body in it," Scout ordered.

Rogers carried Nathan Hale from the wagon and instead of dumping him in the hole, gently slid him into it. He looked at Scout. "Do you want to say any words?"

"He spoke the words that needed to be said better than anything I could conjure up," Scout said. "Bury him."

Rogers was faster filling the hole in. When he was done, there was small man-shaped mound of raw dirt.

Rogers looked around. "Don't suppose you want to mark it?"

Scout shook her head.

"He'll be lost then," Rogers said. He walked to the wagon and slid the shovel back in the barrel. Scout noted that his hands were raw and bleeding from the work, but he didn't complain.

"We're all lost," Scout said. "His last words will be long remembered." She looked at Rogers. "No one will ever know where you're buried."

Rogers gave her a sharp look. "You're gonna kill me then?"

"No," Scout said. "You have some years left, but they'll be miserable ones. You'll spend time as a prisoner. You'll be forced to leave the Colonies and your wife will divorce you so she can stay here in the new country that will become after Washington is victorius. You'll die alone and a pauper in England. No one will know what happens to your body."

"You sound as if you know that," Rogers said.

"I do. That's why I'm not killing you even though I very much want to." Scout turned and walked away, leaving Rogers alone with the soon-to-be forever lost grave of Nathan Hale.

And then she was in the tunnel of time.

She allowed herself to be carried along. She was listless,

exhausted from the mission and the death of one so young and innocent.

Nathan Hale's words would be recorded in various forms and repeated by many during the war and afterward. Novel and inspiring, but Scout found little in them to savor. She knew the context under which they'd been spoken.

She looked about, at the grey walls of the tunnel. At first there was nothing to see, no other possibilities. But then, to the left, she was a flickering image. It was black and white, like an old film. General Washington at the head of a column of soldiers. Marching hard along a wagon track through a thick forest.

An ambush. Redcoats firing, decimating the Colonist ranks. Close quarters fighting. Bayonets, muskets used as clubs, fists and rocks. Washington wielding his sword. Striking down the first of the swarm of red that surrounded him, then disappearing in it.

The scene shifted to Washington on a scaffold on Wall Street in New York City. The same place he was supposed to be sworn in as the first President of the United States in 1789. Standing on the scaffold nearby is Colonel Robert Rogers and General Howe. Unlike Hale, he is given a drop. In the harbor, a victorious British fleet fires salute after salute.

Blackness.

Did this mean there was a timeline where Rogers plan worked? Or was it just a Possibility that she had thwarted? Who knew?

However, instead of arriving at the Possibility Palace, she was slowing. Scout felt as if she were suspended into a cloud of grey nothingness.

"Great," she said as she waited to see what came next.

SALEM, MASSACHUSETTS. 22 September 1692

"No, you will not, young lady," Pandora snapped. "That is not what the Sight is for."

"Thank you for saving me," Unity Hale said. Then she walked into the gathering dawn, toward Salem.

Lara and Pandora stood side by side, impressed and confused.

"Well," Pandora said, but there was nothing more.

"We know she doesn't do it," Lara said.

"What?"

"Because I already saved her from being pressed a few weeks from now," Lara said.

Pandora shook her head. "That's not how it works. If Unity Hale dies today, that mission is voided."

"But it happened."

"Lara, you—"

Lara held up a hand. "I know, I know. The vagaries of the variables."

"Excuse me?" Pandora said.

"Come on," Lara said. "Her heart's in the right place. Her mind, I'm not so sure about."

Pandora strode next to Lara on the path to Salem. "She is powerful."

"That's what I'm afraid of."

"But she's still evolving," Pandora said, hurrying to keep up as Lara picked up the pace. "It is not fully formed."

"Meaning?"

"Meaning that when I channeled through her to stop the attackers, I sensed her power but also her weakness."

Lara shifted into a jog as she spotted Unity's slight figure ahead on the trail. "And?"

They were almost upon Unity, who glanced over her shoulder and started sprinting.

"Frak," Lara muttered. She went all out and her longer legs allowed her to catch the girl and jump on her.

The two tumbled to the dirt. Unity fought like a wildcat, scratching and squirming, trying to break free. Lara almost lost her, then Pandora was there. The two of them pinned the much lighter girl to the ground.

"Get off me."

Both older women felt the literal impact of that command and if they had been anyone else, they might have let her go.

Lara stared into Unity's eyes. "We can't let you sacrifice yourself.

Unity stopped squirming. "One life for eight. It's the right thing to do."

"It's not what happens," Lara said.

"They're not guilty," Unity said. "It's all lies. All of it. Neighbor turning on neighbor. Some for money. Some for land. Some for a slight from the past. Most to save themselves. They've all lost their minds. But some of it also because of me. Because I tried to help people in ways they couldn't understand. I must pay for what I've caused."

Pandora spoke. "You can't save them, girl. You have to take care of youself." The 'goddess' kept one hand on Unity and gripped one of Lara's hands

Lara could feel Pandora's power. She stared with Pandora into Unity's eyes. They could sense the determination to do good, to sacrifice to save the eight condemned. As powerful, perhaps more so, was the overwhelming guilt. They saw visions of Unity using her power in small, and sometimes large, ways. It was under- standable how her interference in the 'natural' order would cause problems. Sick people at death's door recovered in ways that couldn't be explained. Wrongs were righted, but in doing so, Unity caused a ripple effect throughout the town that built on itself until people were confused. And confused people often became frightened. And frightened people became angry. And angry people . . .

Lara looked over at Pandora. The Salem Witch Trials *were*, to a large degree, Unity's fault.

"She was not the executioner," Pandora said as she spread her fingers over Unity's forehead and the girl's eyes closed and she slipped into unconsciousness.

Together they worked to suppress the urge, to break it into pieces that would tumble away. It was as if they were tearing apart a logjam of determination, ripping away one stick at a time. It was hard and tedious work and the clock was ticking.

Unity opened her eyes. "I will not let you."

Lara felt the surge of power from the young girl, a blast of heat that washed over her. They were losing her, losing the battle.

Pandora suddenly gasped in pain.

Lara looked up and saw a Lukas standing behind the 'goddess', twisting the knife he'd slammed into her back.

Lara leapt up, wrapping both arms around Lukas. They fell to the ground, as she whipped out her own dagger and plunged it into his chest. There was a smile on his lips as he dissipated into dust.

Lara turned. Unity was kneeling over Pandora, who was gasping for breath. Dark blood was frothing around her mouth.

Lara knelt on the other side and turned the 'goddess' on her side to check the wound. She put pressure on it, but the blood pulsed through her fingers.

"The forever death," Pandora said. "Who'd have thought? Here? This place? Now?" She shook her head in disbelief.

"You'll be all right," Lara said. "Open a gate. Can't your people help you?"

"I can feel the wound," Pandora gasped. "Too deep."

"Lie still," Unity said.

"Good," Lara said. "Help her stay calm."

But that wasn't what Unity was doing. She put her hands over Lara's. Looked at her. "Let me."

Lara removed the pressure on the wound, allowing Unity to take over.

Pandora's eyes widened in surprise. "Oh!"

Lara looked at Unity's blood covered hands. They were surrounded by a blue glow. There was sweat on Unity's brow and she was breathing hard. Lara got up and went behind the young girl and wrapped her arms around Unity's slight frame, giving her all the support, she could. She felt her own strength being drawn away, into the girl, into Pandora.

The three remained like that for several minutes until suddenly Unity gasped, her hands dropping away and she went limp in Lara's arms. The wound wasn't bleeding.

Lara carefully lowered the girl to the forest floor. Checked her breathing to confirm she was alive. Then looked at Pandora. The 'goddess' sat up. She felt around her body, to her back.

"She healed me."

"She's out cold," Lara said.

"She has such power," Pandora said. She stood, gathering her Naga staff from where Lara had dropped it. "I wonder whether Scout . . ." she didn't finish.

There was the sound of voices not far away, hushed but also excited at the prospect of pending death.

Lara looked up. "Dawn has come."

In the light of a new day, they could see through the edge of the forest to the village where a crowd had gathered around the gallows. They were surrounded by an ugly black/red aura in Lara's sight.

"Will Unity remember this?" Lara asked.

Pandora knelt next to Unity and put her hands on the child's head. "Her power is recuperating. It took almost all of it out of her. If she goes too far one day, she will not recover." She closed her eyes in concentration. "No. She won't remember you or I."

They both looked as the crowd went silent. A man dressed in

black was shouting something, reading from a leather-bound book, but the words were indistinguishable at this distance.

Eight people were lifted up one by one and stood on the wooden plank held up by two saw horses. Another man on a ladder was moving along the line, slipping a black hood over each as they were brought up, along with a noose from the gallows pole. Several of them were sobbing. One was protesting, although the words didn't reach. The others seemed resigned to their fate.

Unity began to stir and Lara put her hand on the girl's forehead. "Rest a little longer." And Unity slumped back.

The man in black finished reading, closing the book. He nodded at the two men, one standing next to each sawhorse. They swung heavy sledges, knocking them out from the supporting plank. And the condemned.

The drop wasn't enough to kill. The bodies spasmed and jerked and then . . .

Then Lara is in tunnel of time as the last of the victims of the Salem Witch Trials suffered their fate as history dictated. She could still feel Unity's cool forehead on the skin of her blood-covered palm.

She became aware that she was in a gray nothingness. There was no sense of movement as there had been before.

In the weightlessness of timelessness, Lara leaned back and let her body relax.

Whatever was going to happen would.

WASHINGTON D.C.. 22 September 1862

Lincoln put the cup of tea to the side. Turned the penny over in his long fingers, looked up at Eagle once more. "What you are suggesting is preposterous."

"He is lying, sir," the Keep said. "He showed up today and has been spinning tales since he arrived."

"That might be," Lincoln said. He held up the penny. "This could easily be made, although the work is excellent. A parlor trick that—"

Eagle dared to interrupt. "'*Yes! I'm prepared, through endless night, to take that fiery berth! Think not with tales of hell to fright Me, who am dammed on earth! Sweet steel! Come forth from out your sheath, And glistening, speak your powers. Rip up the organs of my breath, and draw my blood in showers! I strike! It quivers in that heart which drives me to this end; I draw and kiss the bloody dart. My last— my only friend*'!"

"Where did you read that?" Lincoln demanded.

"Where you sent it," Eagle replied. "The Sangamo Journal in 1841."

"I wrote no such thing," Lincoln said.

"A.A. Springs," Eagle said.

The effect on the President was electric. "Get out," he snapped at the Keep. "I need to speak to this man in private."

The Keep opened her mouth to protest, but Lincoln pointed a long finger. "Out."

Eagle opened the door as the Keep wheeled herself out. He shut the door behind her and faced the President.

"A.A. Springs is a secret in my family. Whatever you may think you know of the man; he is *not* my father."

"I did not say he was, sir," Eagle said.

"How do you know the name?" Lincoln demanded.

"My people know many secrets," Eagle said.

"You know things," Lincoln said, "but they are of the past." He held up the penny. "This is not of the past. It portends to be of the future. You claim you have knowledge that the Proclamation *must* be announced today. How do you know that?"

"My people have those who can see—"

Lincoln waved off the story. "The truth."

"I come from the future."

Surprisingly, Lincoln nodded. "Jefferson suspected it. He said he had dreams in 1776 while writing the Declaration of Independence. That three of the Committee of Five had the exact same dream of the future. At least three would admit to having it. That the visitor that came to them was dark-skinned. Not a Negro but one from the Far East. And he had a signed copy of the Declaration of Independence before it had been signed. Which, of course, is impossible. But it was there in front of them."

"His name was Doc," Eagle said.

Lincoln continued. "This stranger was the one who proposed getting the Declaration of Emancipation signed but then hidden and delayed fifty years. Jefferson wrote that Franklin saw the practicality of it immediately. They agreed. Then the stranger said that a woman would show up in fifty years at Monticello. And she did. Looking exactly as described. Something that should be impossible but she was there in front of him. I read the words in the Book of Truths. I have pondered them often. Trying to understand. Visitors from the future were one possibility that had all the trapping of making sense except for the very act itself. How do you do it?"

"I wouldn't be able to explain it, Mister President," Eagle said. "Except understand that we are in a larger war. The people of this world against an enemy that seeks to destroy us all by changing our history. You must announce the Emancipation Proclamation today because that is what happened in our history in the future."

Lincoln interlaced his fingers and leaned back in the chair. "Amazing. Of course, if I accept your premise, then there is much you know that I would like to know."

"I've already violated my oath by telling you the truth," Eagle said.

"You know when my wife dies?"

"Yes, sir."

"Does she pass before me?"

Eagle hesitated. "No, sir."

Lincoln was pained. "She will not bear me going first very well. And you know the date and means of my death?"

"Yes, sir. But I—"

Lincoln held up a hand. "No, no. That is knowledge no man could bear to live with. No pun intended. We win the war?"

"Yes, sir."

"That is sufficient," Lincoln said. "Will there be much more blood?"

"I'm afraid so, sir."

"One more question, if you please."

"Sir, I have said too much."

"Grant," Lincoln said. "I want to bring him east. Should I?" He smiled sadly. "Or should I phrase it: Do I?"

"Yes, sir."

"I will not press you any further. Does the Keep know your true nature?"

"No, sir."

"Interesting," Lincoln said. "What do you make of her?"

Eagle was confused. "She keeps the Book of Truths. There is always one in the White House."

"And the job?"

"To maintain the Book of Truths, sir."

"Bring her in, please," Lincoln said.

Eagle went to the door and opened it. The Keep was just outside. She rolled in.

As soon as the door was closed, Lincoln said: "I will make the announcement today."

"Sir!" The Keep said. "I beg you to—"

Lincoln silenced her with a single raised finger. "You have been spinning tales to me for a while. I feel it in your voice. The power behind the words, trying to bend me to your will. My wife warned me of it. There are many who think my wife a fool, but she is the smartest woman I have ever met. I knew it from the first day I met her. Your words of comfort to her have so much power they can still the voices in her head. No one has ever been able to do that for her."

"I try to help," the Keep said.

"I think you do more than that," Lincoln said. "It has not passed unnoticed that you do with my wife what no other could, least of all by her. And, like this coin—" he turned the penny in the light—"there are two sides to that talent. You have been pushing me to delay the announcement of the Proclamation. I must wonder why, since once I am out of your presence, your arguments wilt. But while you are in the room and speaking, they make sense."

"I am only trying to help," the Keep said.

"But that is not your position," Lincoln said. "I have more advisors than there are leaves on the trees. Your position is to keep the Book, not write it."

Eagle finally understood. He reached for the dagger secreted inside his jacket as the Keep leapt up out of her chair, pulling her own dagger from inside her petticoat.

Eagle's only advantage was that the wheelchair pushed backward as she rose, causing her to stumble. He slashed, the tip of the blade slicing her on the left side of the face. Blood pulsed forth, but she was focused on the President. Encumbered by the heavy layers of clothing, she wasn't as fast as she should have been.

Eagle slammed the dagger into her back with all his strength while he grabbed her gray hair with the other, pulling her head back.

The wig ripped off in his hand, revealing short, dark hair.

She was still trying for the President, bringing the dagger up for a strike when she died, disintegrating into dust, leaving empty clothing.

"I did not suspect *that*," Lincoln said, surprisingly calm given what had just happened. "Although I suspected the person for a long time. Where did she go?"

"To nothingness," Eagle said, tossing aside the wig, which was of this time and place.

"She was from this enemy you spoke of?"

"Yes, sir." Eagle knew now what he had missed beneath the wig and the heavy make up and the layers of clothing. "She was a Lara."

"A what?"

Eagle shook his head. "It wouldn't make sense if I tried to explain. She was trying to change history and when you saw through it, she took drastic action. She must have replaced the Keep sometimes and--"

But then Eagle was in the tunnel of time

AREA 51. 22 September 1947

Moms was in a time tunnel similar to that by which one returned from a mission, but different. She definitely wasn't returning to the Possibility Palace and that was a good thing because she had both hands gripping the fin at the rear of Fat Man.

She could see the demon core tumbling in the vague gray ahead and off to the left along with several scientists. Colonel Thorn had a hand on the cart, but then it and Fat Man separated. Thorn was yelling something but it was eerily silent.

A split appeared ahead in the time tunnel. A divergence in possibilities, but in this case, realities and destinations.

Moms had no control over her path. Thorn, still holding the cart, the scientists and the demon core disappeared into their own time tunnel to the left, hopefully to come back in the future, Moms' past.

Moms went with Fat Man to the right.

. . .

BERLIN, 22 September 1948

Neeley's finger twitched as a Rift crackled into existence. She'd have fired but instantly recognized the large, human figure holding a Naga staff.

"My God!" Neeley ran forward and flung her arms around Roland.

Roland easily lifted her in his embrace as she buried her head in his shoulder.

"Are you all right?" Roland asked. He let go of her and looked her over. "Your wrist?"

"It's bandaged. It'll heal."

Roland looked around. "Where are we?"

"Underneath Tempelhof," Neeley said. She didn't think there was time to do much explaining. "Something is coming. A Rift. Another Rift," she amended.

"Fireflies?" Roland said, standing next to her, Naga staff at the ready.

"There was a Yeti," Neeley said.

Roland frowned. "Through a Rift? That's different." He shook his head. "Everything's a little crazy."

"Are *you* all right?" Neeley asked.

Roland nodded. "Sure. All I did was haul stuff for some old lady. To a bunch of timelines. It was weird. And I don't remember exactly how many so Dane is gonna get a bit pissed during the debrief. Gold plates."

"An 'old lady'?"

"One of the Fates," Roland said. He brightened. "Hey! I killed a Chimera. And you killed a Yeti! That's cool."

"I had help," Neeley said.

"But you're still standing," Roland said. "That's all that counts."

The air crackled and a Rift opened. Roland lifted the Naga staff and Neeley had the forty-five raised.

"Hold!" Neeley yelled at Roland as Angus and Ivar arrived, stumbling into the chamber.

"Hello, lass," Angus said, taking in his new surroundings.

Ivar was dazed and staggered a few steps before collapsing to his knees.

"Where are we?" Angus asked, reaching down and helping Ivar to his feet.

"Berlin," Neeley updated them. "1948. We're underneath Tempelhof."

"Why?" Ivar asked. "Why are we here?"

"Something's coming," Neeley said. She pointed at the radios. "I think the Shadow is going to use those to crash planes from the airlift. Send them the wrong homing signals."

"Can't let that happen to our brave flyboys now, can we?" Angus said. He drew his Naga dagger.

IN THE TUNNEL OF TIME

Scout sensed a presence, a voice, distantly echoing. "Hello?" she called out and feeling quite foolish right after doing it.

Her voice didn't bounce back to her, but was absorbed completely in the tunnel of time. She turned, even though she was floating. All she had to do was think it and her body adjusted position. There was something outside her tunnel. Pressing up against it.

"Hello?" Scout tried again. She went closer to the wall. A single point, not very large. Pressure from the other side.

It took her a moment, then she realized it was a hand. She didn't hesitate. She reached out and pressed her own hand against the wall of the tunnel at that spot.

She experienced the shock of recognition. "Lara!"

. . .

BERLIN, 22 September 1948

A gate opened wide and half-dozen Legion stepped through.

A pair were dead immediately as Neeley fired twice. Roland sliced off the head of a third. Angus slit the throat of one and grabbed another who was headed for Ivar. The Legion slammed his dagger into Angus' lower chest while the old man gutted him.

Neeley finished off the last one and as quickly as it had started, all six were dust.

"Angus is wounded!" Ivar yelled.

Angus looked at the hole in his body where the dagger had dissolved. "Nothing serious." A light froth of blood on his lips when he spoke belied the comment.

"Sucking chest wound," Roland said, putting a supporting arm around Angus. "Lay down."

But before Angus could comply, the air crackled and a red line appeared in the air in the center of the chamber. They scrambled away, readying weapons once more.

The red line widened and a Rift over twenty feet wide by the same high, hovered a foot above the pitted concrete floor of the chamber. The Rift was filled with utter darkness.

Once more, Roland had the Naga at the ready. Neeley aimed her forty-five. Angus hefted his Naga dagger and even Ivar drew his.

Despite their readiness, they were not prepared as Fat Man dropped out of the Gate onto the floor with resounding thud, cracking the concrete. Moms landing on top of it was almost an after-thought. She tumbled to the floor, her breath knocked out and lay there gasping to regain it.

"Hell of an entrance," Neeley said to Moms as she helped the team leader to her feet. "Tell me it's not armed."

"I think it's armed," Moms said, trying to catch her breath.

"Then it has to be on a delay initiator," Roland said.

"What are you all doing here?" Moms asked as she got oriented. "What am I doing here?"

Angus was on the floor of the chamber, not to deal with his wound as Roland had suggested, but scooting underneath the forward edge of the bomb where a control panel was bolted, but it was protected by thick, blast-proof glass. Angus found the wire for the initiator. It had snapped an inch out of the glass; after Thorn had pressed the red button.

"Analog," Angus said, peering at the clock inside that was winding down. "Old school. But, yes, it's armed."

At its core, Fat Man had a sphere of plutonium 239, surrounded by blocks of high explosive that were designed to go off symmetrically and implode the plutonium to critical density. That would set off the nuclear chain reaction.

"How long?" Moms asked.

"Two minutes, thirty seconds until detonation," Angus replied, running his hands around the panel. He tried to pry off the covering but it was solidly attached and hard to get at since the bomb was upside down from how it had been.

Roland and Moms got down, lying on the floor on either side of him to help in any way they could.

"We could run?" Ivar suggested.

"You ain't outrunning this, laddie," Angus said, slapping the side of the bomb, causing everyone but Roland to wince. "Your spear, boy," he said to Roland. "Put the point here." He indicted the seam between the bomb and panel cover.

Roland did as ordered.

"Leverage," Angus said.

Roland put all his muscle into it. Moms and Neeley joined in, but there was only so much room to get a hand in.

"Two minutes."

. . .

IN THE TUNNEL OF TIME

Scout's hand pushed through the wall of the tunnel. She grasped Lara's hand and felt the grip returned. Both pulled and the tunnels shuddered, neither pulling through to the other. Instead, the tunnels merged into one.

"That was weird," Scout said. She looked her friend over. "You all right?"

"I'm fine," Lara said. "You?"

"Bummed. Had to watch Nathan Hale hang."

Lara nodded. "They hung eight in Salem. Unity wanted to save them."

"Oh," Scout said. "That sucks," she understated.

"Why aren't we back?" Lara asked.

"I don't know," Scout said. She looked both ways in the tunnel. "Usually, I just get pulled to the Possibility Palace. You know. You've done it."

"We're paused for a reason," Lara said. "Give me your hands."

The two young women gripped hands, focusing.

"Moms," Scout said.

"Neeley," Lara said at the same time.

"And Roland," Scout added. "Same place. That's not right."

Lara let go of Scout and pointed. "This way."

BERLIN, 22 September 1948

"Maybe it won't go off," Roland hoped. "Maybe going through the Gate messed it up?"

"Clocks still moving," Neeley noted, looking past his shoulder.

"The Shadow diverted me to this time and place," Moms said.

"The Russians test their first nuclear weapon next year," Neeley said. "There will be no doubting this came from the U.S.. God knows how people will react to most of Berlin getting wiped out."

"Can you let us focus?" Angus said, his voice mild.

The blast proof cover moved the slightest bit

"That's it," Angus said. "Keep the pressure."

"But the mission is over," Neeley murmured, more to herself.

ABOVE THEM, in the tunnel of time, Lara turned to Scout. "We have to save them."

"If our missions are complete," Scout said, "we should be getting pulled back to the Possibility Palace."

Look!" Lara pointed.

Outside of the tunnel, a thick black circle was approaching fast.

"The return," Scout said.

ROLAND'S MUSCLES BULGED. He was fortunate that he was using a Naga staff as leverage; regular metal would have snapped.

"You're getting it, lad," Angus said in a calm voice, lying on his back, his Leatherman in hand, ready.

The clock passed into the final minute, the black minutes hand on zero, the red second hand sweeping around.

"SOMETHING'S WRONG," Lara said.

"Yeah, they got a big bomb in there," Scout said. "We gotta get them out of there before it goes off."

Lara was looking at the rapidly approaching time tunnel and then into the chamber floating below them.

THE HEAVY BULLETPROOF glass popped off and Roland, Moms and Neeley went sprawling. Angus was focused on the panel. The second hand ticked second after second. Angus traced the initiating wire to a small access plate. He pried it open rather than waste time on the screws.

Then the tunnel of time hit and Moms, Neeley, Roland, Ivar and Angus were sucked into it.

Along with Fat Man.

THE RETURN

W ASHINGTON D.C.. 22 September 1862
Eagle flowed through the tunnel. There were different possibilities on all sides, too many to keep track.

One where Lincoln didn't announce the Emancipation Proclamation, but apparently took Jefferson Davis' offer of reconciliation, most likely with the edging of the false Keep. The country never came together. There were flashes of border wars that kept getting more intense, until there was a final Civil War, but the result of that was gone as Eagle moved faster and faster.

He caught glimpses of a funeral procession for Lincoln in another timeline; years too soon. Was that the one where Lincoln accused the Keep and he didn't stop her blade in time? That image of the procession exploded into black and red with no detail and Eagle was glad he didn't see any more of it.

And then he was back, at the Possibility Palace.

But no one else was.

Yet.

· · ·

BERLIN. 22 September 1948

"Time?" Moms yelled to Angus, who was holding on to Fat Man with one hand, still working on the panel with the other.

"Good news," Angus said, his lips flecked with blood. "She's stopped."

They all turned as Scout and Lara appeared in the tunnel.

"Because we're between times," Lara said. "It will start up once we reach our destination."

Outside the tunnel they were flashing forward, toward the Possibility Palace.

"That was the plan," Moms realized. "Destroy the Palace. We have to stop it."

"Working on it," Angus said.

"There's no time," Lara said, looking over her shoulder. "We'll be there in a few seconds."

"We can't just—" Moms began, but Scout pre-empted whatever she was about to say by diving forward to a point next to Angus, below the bomb. She gripped the sides of the tunnel and spread her arms, ripping asunder the integrity, opening up to a timeline flickering below. She reached toward Angus, who understood.

The old man gripped Scout's hand and then, in the weightlessness of the time tunnel, pulled the bomb with him. He, and the bomb, were gone, out of the tunnel, passing by Scout who let go of the tear.

A moment later there was a bright flash behind them, outside of the tunnel.

And then Scout, Moms, Neeley, Ivar, Roland and Lara returned home to the Possibility Palace.

AFTERMATH

The Possibility Palace

    Eagle finished carving Angus' name into the table in the team room.

It is protocol for us to acknowledge the death of a team member because no one else will," Moms said. "We must pay our respects and give honors."

The surviving team members linked hands in a circle around the table along with Orlando, Sin Fen and Dane.

"He never received a name from the team," Moms said. She glanced at Orlando. "Not that he would have accepted any but his own. Angus. His past was complicated. Many years of proud service in the British Special Air Service. Further work for covert operations for his country. Warrant Officer Angus McTiernay has made the ultimate sacrifice for his country, for his world, and for mankind. We speak his rank and his name as it was."

They all spoke together: "Warrant Officer Angus McTiernay."

Orlando spoke: "As long as a name is remembered, we live on."

Every member of the team nodded.

Moms continued. "We, the Time Patrol, have seen many things

and been to many places, and many times. We don't know the limits of science, and we don't know the limits of the soul. If there is some life after this, or some existence on a plane we can't conceive of, then know our teammate is there, in a good place. Because that is what he deserves for performing his duty without any acknowledgement, and for making the ultimate sacrifice. If there is nothingness in death, then he is in his final peace and will not be troubled any more by the nightmares of this world."

"I hope and pray," Orlando said, "that he is with his son once more. He loved his son more than anything in the world."

"There will be no medals," Eagle said. "Either from the United States or his own country. But if those who gave medals knew, they certainly would award him the highest possible. He saved the Possibility Palace and the Time Patrol. And by saving the Patrol he saved our timeline."

"All we can do," Scout said, "is keep him in our hearts."

"He saved the world," Lara said. "A lot," she murmured to herself.

Orlando pulled his flask out and took a sip. "To Angus."

He passed it to the Time Patrol member next to him.

The End

For Now

OUR HISTORY AFTERWARD

NEW YORK CITY, 22 September 1776
Nathan Hale graduated Yale in 1773. He was a schoolteacher. He joined the Continental Army in 1775 during the Siege of Boston.

Nathan Hale's body has never been found.

In 1776 Robert Rogers formed the Queen's Rangers. He was forced into retirement by the British Army in 1777 for 'poor health'. Because of his service for the Crown, George Washington got the New Hampshire Legislature to pass two decrees against him, including a divorce for his wife who remained in the Colonies. Rogers tried to raise a Ranger unit in Canada but failed because of his acute alcoholism. He was briefly captured by an American privateer and spent time in prison in New York before escaping and going to England. He died in obscurity and debt in London in 1795. His grave is unknown.

BERLIN. 22 September 1948

On June 24, 1948, the Soviet Union blocked all road and rail travel to and from West Berlin, cutting off the city from outside supplies. On June 26, 1948, the first planes took off from bases in

England and western Germany and landed in West Berlin. It was a daunting logistical task to provide food, clothing, water, medicine, and other necessities of life for the over 2 million citizens of the city. For nearly a year, American and British planes landed around the clock. In total, the United States delivered 1,783,572.7 tons. The British delivered 541,936.9 tons. This totaled 2.3 Million tons from 277, 569 total flights to Berlin. C-47's and C-54's alone traveled over 92 million miles in order to do so. A total of 101 fatalities were recorded as a result of the operation, including 31 Americans, mostly due to crashes.

SALEM, MASSACHUSETTS. 22 September 1692 A.D.

Salem, MA was settled in 1629 and named Salem, for Shalom, a Hebrew word meaning 'place of peace'.

The first accusations of witchcraft occurred in January 1692. As the year went accusations and counter-accusations flew. The first hanging occurred on 10 June. All told 19 people are hanged with the last eight taking place on the Equinox. One, Giles Corey, was pressed to death because he refused to confess, because that would allow the states to seize all his property from his family. He last words were "More weight."

MANCHESTER, NEW YORK. 22 September 1823 A.D.

According to Latter Day Saint belief, the golden plates are the source from which Joseph Smith translated the Book of Mormon, a sacred text of the faith.

WASHINGTON D.C.. 22 September 1862

A.A. Springs is the name of a man rumored to have been Abraham Lincoln's true father. His mother became pregnant while visiting North Carolina and Mister Springs. Most historians discount this.

The African Burial Ground is a National Monument in New York City.

. . .

THE NIGHTSTALKERS ENCOUNTERED the modern Keep and the Book of Truths in *Nightstalkers: The Book of Truths.*

An excerpt from Area 51: Invasion follows Author information.

I've just updated The Green Beret Preparation and Survival Guide. If you email me at bob@bobmayer.com I'd be glad to send you a free copy of the checklists from the book in Kindle format (mobi). You can also download for free from my web site on my Freebies page.

Stay safe!

ABOUT THE AUTHOR

Thanks for the read!
If you enjoyed the book, please leave a review as they are very important and greatly appreciated.

Bob is a NY Times Bestselling author, graduate of West Point and former Green Beret. He's had over 80 books published including the #1 series The Green Berets, The Cellar, Area 51, Shadow Warriors, Atlantis, and the Time Patrol. Born in the Bronx, having traveled the world (usually not tourist spots), he now lives peacefully with his wife and dogs.
For information on all his books, please get a free copy of the *Reader's Guide*. You can download it in mobi (Amazon) ePub (iBooks, Nook, Kobo) or PDF, from his home page at www. bobmayer.com

For free eBooks, short stories and audio short stories, please go to
http://bobmayer.com/freebies/
The page includes free and discounted book constantly updated.
There are also free shorts stories and free audiobook stories.
There are over 220 free, downloadable Powerpoint presentations
via Slideshare on a wide range of topics from history, to survival,
to writing, to book trailers. This page and slideshows are
constantly updated at:
http://bobmayer.com/workshops/
Questions, comments, suggestions: Bob@BobMayer.com
Blog: http://bobmayer.com/blog/
Twitter: https://twitter.com/Bob_Mayer
Facebook: https://www.facebook.com/authorbobmayer
Instagram: https://www.instagram.com/sifiauthor/
Youtube: https://www.youtube.com/user/IWhoDaresWins
Subscribe to his newsletter for the latest news, free eBooks,
audio, etc.

All fiction is here: **Bob Mayer's Fiction**
All nonfiction is here: **Bob Mayer's Nonfiction**

AREA 51: INVASION

MARFA, TEXAS

"Damn it, Darlene! I told you not to watch that fake news. There aint no such thing as aliens. All of this has been bullshit so the government can come get my guns. Turn it off. And get your damn dog off the couch."

"I don't think so," Darlene muttered watching the images from Russia and the massive alien spaceship. "That's a lot of work just to come and get your guns, Bobby."

Thin, almost starved-looking, Darlene had badly dyed reddish hair self-cut shaggy short. Her arms scrolled with tattoos. She wore ripped jeans and a red t-shirt with the Marine Corps emblem on the front. She was sitting cross-legged on the nice leather couch, Bobby's only legacy from his stepmom, peering at the TV. It was all kinda confusing cause some of the feeds would go blank and the news folk were scrambling to figure things out.

One hand absently scratched Rex's head. The dog was a mutt, something German Shepherd/Chow/Mexico street fighter. She'd found him wandering about a few months ago and viewed him as a good luck charm and more trustworthy companion than her quasi-boyfriend of expediency.

Bobby didn't like bad news, or fake news as he called it. "I told you to turn the damn thing off!" He grabbed his AR-15 off the pegs by the door to the trailer, single-wide, but some day she'd dreamed of double-wide as long as she had to stay here. Looked like that dream wasn't gonna come. All bad things must end.

"Don't you dare!" Darlene yelled as Bobby leveled the rifle at the TV.

It had a fancy sniper scope that had cost a week and a half of her waitressing tips and initiated a terrible row between the two of them as Darlene didn't see the need, given Bobby only shot cans, plus he didn't even know how to zero it in. The fight had been more a drunken brawl, followed by reasonably decent make-up sex. That still didn't make up for the money, but it didn't seem that was going to matter now either.

Bobby fired four rounds, fast as he could pull the trigger, blasting the screen.

"Great shooting, numb-nuts," Darlene said. "Shoulda saved your ammo. I think we're gonna need it." She didn't point out he hadn't needed that damn, stupid scope to hit the TV. Rex growled at Bobby. "Easy," Darlene said. "Now aint the time for our plan. Gotta wait boy."

"That plan thing aint never funny," Bobby said. "You and that damn dog."

"Why do you think it's a joke?" Darlene stomped out of the trailer in her heavy black boots, Rex at her heel. She stood in the 'front yard' comprising of desert and pulled the smokes out of roll on the left arm of her t-shirt.

"You should quit," Bobby said from inside the nebulous safety of the ripped screen door, but his voice was a bit subdued, as it always was after he did something stupid, which was much more often than Darlene liked.

"Don't matter now," Darlene said, staring out over the desolate west Texas landscape. "Shoulda bought that double-wide, Bobby, when I told you to. At least we'd have been going out happier."

EARTH ORBIT

While the massive Swarm Battle Core settled into high orbit, 20,000 miles above the Earth's surface, the results of the Metamorphosis were walking, crawling, swimming, slithering, stalking and winging their way to designated warships for the pending drop on the planet.

The Core's orbit was opposite the planet's rotation. For the first go-around, the Core was traversing the northern hemisphere, just above the Tropic of Capricorn as data indicated it would be the source of most Scale opposition. Weapons systems on the surface of the Core were powered up.

It was all standing operating procedure for a reaping.

Even 20,000 miles up, the sphere was massive. Six thousand miles wide at the center and four thousand at the polar axis, it was much larger, and much, much closer, than the moon. As the Core orbited the planet, it began targeting procedures to negate potential threats prior to drop. Numerous sites had already been determined due to intercepts across the array of electromagnetic transmissions from the planet. More would be determined as the Scale life, in this case humans, reacted.

There was no rush.

The result was inevitable.

RAVEN ROCK, PENNSYLVANIA

"Too high," Marshal Krasmav complained to General Clark, the Russian's voice crackling from static. "My missiles do not have the range. And unless my intelligence services have been greatly mistaken all these years, neither do yours."

"I have always enjoyed your sense of humor, Sergei," the American Chairwoman of the Joint Chiefs, said. "You maintain it even now, which is admirable. We know we have both violated that treaty. A vertical launch will work. The booster will run out of fuel before reaching the target, but if aimed correctly, inertia will send the warheads onward."

"Ah, my dear General," Krasmav responded, "you know me well. But if we do that, then we have to fire to intercept as the Core comes overheard, in volleys. We will not be able to concentrate our power."

"It's all we have," Clark responded. "The good news is the detonations should be far enough from the atmosphere to avoid radiation. I'm sending the launch profiles my people have worked out for both of us. Wait one." She pointed at one of her staff.

She waited as the information was transmitted. General Clark was one of the first female graduates of the Military Academy so many years ago. Now she was the first female Chief of Staff. She was located in the Pentagon's emergency command and control bunker deep under Raven Rock Mountain in southeast Pennsylvania, not far from the hallowed ground of Gettysburg.

Krasmav, the Russian Chief of the General Staff, finally responded. "You seem very knowledgeable on all my launch sites, missile profiles, and the location of my missile submarines. I am glad we never went to war. It appears, how do you say it, that I get first crack at this?"

"You do," Clark said. "The Core is on path for intercept to your westernmost missiles in two minutes. Can you launch by then?"

"Already sent the order, my friend."

THE RUSSIAN ICBM cluster was close to the border with the Ukraine. It was equipped with SS-X-30 Satan 2 ICBMs, each with ten heavy nuclear warheads. The Core picked up the signature of the first launch in under two seconds. The response was immediate.

As the first Satan cleared its silo, a particle beam accelerator on the surface of the Core fired a burst of energy. The bolt traveled at the speed of light, as opposed to the gathering speed of the Satan's initial rocket booster.

The missile blew up two hundred feet above the launch silo.

The Swarm wasn't content with the lone missile. Additional accelerators fired, obliterating the launch silo and the surrounding terrain for a distance of five miles.

Now recognizing the signature for this particular threat, the Core reacted faster to subsequent launches, hitting Russian missiles upon initial ignition before they cleared the silo.

Then it hit the main base launching them and the adjacent town, slagging all of it.

Data gathered from Scale electromagnetic communications were analyzed by the Swarm and the targeting matrix was updated. Russian military posts and units that didn't have strategic missiles, but could be located due to their broadcasts, were hit as the forward edge of the Battle Core passed overheard.

Transmitting radio and television broadcast stations were also destroyed as the Swarm didn't bother to distinguish the contents of the electromagnetic traffic.

GENERAL CLARK WATCHED the Russian feeds go dark. She could also see via her country's low orbit, spy satellite feeds the destruction on the other side of the globe.

She had the phone to her ear. "Sergei."

"Yes, I am seeing. It's got everything targeted. Everything we have. I do not think you will have any greater fortune with this plan."

Clark checked the main display covering the front wall of the OpCenter. The shadow of the Core was approaching Moscow.

"Can you get out?" she asked Krasmav.

"And go where?" Krasmav replied. "This is my duty post."

The line reached the suburbs of Moscow.

"I can hear detonations," Krasmav said. "I have issued orders for our other facilities to stand down. Perhaps the alien will miss one or two and they can survive this initial onslaught."

The static was getting worse. Clark heard a loud sound in the background noise. "Farewell, my friend."

"Ah," Krasmav said. "Perhaps we will meet in Valhalla."

Clark gripped the phone tighter. "I never took you for a religious man."

"It is not religion," Krasmav said. "It is the place warriors go after fighting bravely."

The line passed over Moscow and the phone went dead.

With the time she had left, General Clark began issuing new orders as the Core continued its deadly eastward track over Russia.

AIRSPACE, WORLDWIDE

Around the world, twenty-six brand new Boeing 777s and 787s originating from Paine Field north of Seattle, began to explode, one by one, as they descended to land at their destinations. The first was over the water on approach to San Francisco International. The second, Denver International. The explosions rippled around the world at major airports, relatively insignificant given the larger issue of the alien Battle Core's arrival.

They all had something else in common besides their origin and having only a pilot and co-pilot on board: they carried a tube of the *Danse Macabre*, a mixture of three extremely lethal viruses. This was all part of a *Myrddin* plan which had been overwhelmed by recent events. Just a footnote in the apocalypse.

Not that the unfortunate pilots of those planes had anticipated the explosions, either. They'd thought they were to land and pass the tube to *Myrddin* agents in the various destinations. However, the Cleansing, part of the original plan to brutally solve issues such as over-population, pollution, climate-change, etcetera in one viral sweep, was no longer important in the big picture.

The *Myrddin* were a rogue group of Watchers, a sect of humans that had watched the alien Airlia presence on Earth for millennia, ever since the destruction of Atlantis. Founded by Merlin, the *Myrddin* had decided that more than watching was needed. Humans needed to act. During the recent rebellion against the Airlia and subsequent World War III, the head of the Myrddin, Mrs. Parrish, had seized the opportunity to implement a plan long in the making called The Strategy. Her plan to load her five thousand Chosen children on the mothership, then spread the *Danse* around the world, cleansing it, and then repopulating it with the Chosen had been overtaken by events when the Swarm Battle Core appeared.

Thus the twenty-six explosions, occurring at population centers around the globe, were just one of a myriad of unfolding disasters and the remnant of an already abandoned plan.

SURVIVAL SILO, KANSAS

Tremble's amplified voice broke through the chatter of the rich and fearful: "We're the safest people on the planet."

The forty-six men, women and children, net worth in excess of 200 billion dollars, all turned toward Tremble. He was flanked by an armed guard, an unnecessary thing at the moment, but as important for calming the herd as his words.

"I promised you," Tremble continued, "and now I am making good on my promise. You made it here. You are in the safest place on the planet." Repetition was key; he'd learned that at a night class he'd taken several years ago.

He was standing at the front of the plush movie theater, on the eighth floor of the Complex, his clients crowded in, all the seats taken and the rest standing. He was a big man, over six and a half feet tall and had played college football, but now most of the muscle had dissolved to fat. Still, his size and confidence impressed this group.

"This silo was designed to take a direct strike from a thermonuclear bomb." Which was a lie, but every business is built on lies. Tremble did firmly believe they were in the safest place, so what was a little white lie?

His assistant stepped up behind, whispering urgently. "The alien ship is attacking Russia from orbit with some sort of ray gun."

Tremble whispered his order. "Close the garage doors."

"The recovery team is still at the airfield with the Beast," the assistant reminded him.

"Close it but be prepared to let the Beast in once it arrives." He faced the crowd and the microphone. "We are now cutting ourselves off from the outside world." He smiled with a confidence he actually felt despite his lies. "We are in the safest place in the world."

EARTH ORBIT

Just after the Swarm Core had entered orbit from above, the captured Airlia Mothership did the same from below, after taking off from Area 51. It held the *Myrddin* vision for mankind's survival in the form of 4,312 specially selected children in deep sleep tubes in its innermost hold.

The Chosen. Not quite at the five thousand planned for, but close enough.

The ruby sphere was in place, powering up the main engine, which would allow the ship to attain Faster Than Light Transit (FTLT).

However, the *Myrddin*, in essence Mrs. Parrish, were no longer in charge of the ship. At the controls of the mile long, cigar shaped alien ship was a former member of the Russian version of Majestic-12, Yakov. The co-pilot was a woman who claimed to be Nikola Tesla's granddaughter, Professor Leahy. The ship was the bounty the human race had taken after defeating the Airlia. And Yakov, Leahy, Nyx and Turcotte had taken it from Mrs. Parrish.

"Do you know how to activate FTLT?" Yakov asked Leahy.

"Hold on." Leahy had her Tesla computer set on the console to the right, her hands on it, eyes closed. The smooth surfaces of the small pyramid shimmered with silver. "It's linking," Leahy said. "I'm linking to the ship."

"Ask it how to go into FTLT," Yakov said, "because I have no idea. And, please, quickly." He looked at the image of the Core rising above the blue-white curvature of the Earth. He tapped the flexpad at his side to call his partner in the war against the aliens. "Mike? Where are you? We can open a hold for you."

"Negative," Mike Turcotte replied over the flexpad from his ship, the *Fynbar*. "I'm staying. Get those people the hell out of here."

A particle beam from the Core hit the mothership. The impact shuddered throughout the craft, the legacy of an alien race, the Airlia, who had been hidden in the Solar System for over ten millennia. The black hull of the mile-long, cigar shaped ship absorbed the hit, but it wouldn't take many more of them, especially with previous damage hastily patched.

"A bit more urgency," Yakov said to Leahy. He leaned toward the flexpad. "Mike? We need you."

MIKE TURCOTTE GLANCED at one of the monitors lining the front of the small spaceship's cockpit. At this altitude he could see the forward edge of the Battle Core to the far west, over the eastern Pacific. He knew more weapons would be brought to bear as the Core closed.

The *Fynbar* was human designed and built, but not of Earth. It had been brought to Earth by two humans who'd been part of a successful planet-wide revolt against the Airlia. They'd planted the seeds of revolt on Earth and overseen it for over 10,000 years. The male had died at the Battle of Camlann during a battle between Airlia proxies posing as Arthur and Mordred. The female, Lisa Duncan had died just recently, crashing the second mothership into the Airlia communication array on Mars, preventing an emergency signal for help from being sent out.

Saucer shaped, the *Fynbar* had a bulge in the forward center and two large pods in the rear, which housed the STL engines. It was dull gray inside and out and designed with two seats inside depressions for pilot and co-pilot in the forward center facing the displays and controls. Turcotte was alone, flying the *Fynbar* in orbit between the mothership and the approaching Core.

Turcotte responded to Yakov. "No. You don't. I'm going back down as soon as you get out of here. What's the hold up?"

"I CAN DO IT," Leahy said, her hands still on the Tesla. She opened her eyes and looked over at Yakov, a bit disoriented from her dual realities, the Tesla link into the mothership's guardian computer still in her mind. "Where should we jump to?"

"Anywhere but here," Yakov said. He glanced at one of the

displays, seeing the tiny *Fynbar* between their location and the massive Core. He whispered a silent prayer.

Leahy closed her eyes.

Darkness fell.

RAVEN ROCK, PENNSYLVANIA

"'The third angel sounded his trumpet, and a great star, blazing like a torch, fell from the sky on a third of the rivers and on the spring of water; the name of the Star is Wormwood. A third of the waters turned bitter, and many people died from the waters that had become bitter'."

"Didn't know you were religious, General," the aide-de-camp said. This bothered the General because the last exchange she'd had with the head of the Russian military, just before he, and everyone with him, had been obliterated, had consisted of her asking him the same question.

"I think a lot of people are converting at the moment," General Clark said.

She, with everyone else in the Raven Rock Emergency Command and Control Center, were watching video feeds from the west coast of the United States as the Swarm Battle Core approached high over the Pacific. As it passed overhead it brought eclipse to a large swath of Earth's surface. She idly wondered how it was affecting the tides. It had already destroyed every Russian ICBM as it passed over EurAsia, negating the plan she'd conjured up with her Russian counterpart to nuke the Core. That triggered one of those strange thoughts that often pop up at the most inappropriate time.

"Did you know that the Ukrainian word for Wormwood is *chornobyl*?" Clark murmured. "I find that odd."

"Excuse me, ma'am?" her aide asked.

"So many strange coincidences," Clark said. "But maybe everything is connected at a level we can't consciously perceive? Maybe we share some sort of genetic memory?"

"I don't know, ma'am."

"I think this is bigger than we know," she murmured. "What was it Turcotte called the Swarm? The Ancient Enemy?"

Several of the center staff were praying. Others were desperately trying to get an outside line, to say last goodbyes.

But no one had deserted. Clark felt a moment's pride at the discipline.

"Status of the boomers?" she asked her aide as she watched the Core's inevitable approach.

"Pacific and Atlantic running silent and deep."

"Do we know if the Core has fired on any of the Pacific subs yet?"

"We have no contact."

"Seventh Fleet?" Clark asked.

"The *Reagan* and all other ships have gone dark."

"Hawaii?" Clark asked.

"Joint Base Pearl Harbor-Hickam is—" her aide paused, trying to find a way to speak the unspeakable—"gone. Along with Schofield Barracks and Marine Base Kaneohe."

Clark asked: "Silos?"

"Launches have been aborted, blast doors closed. Authorization has been disseminated to LCC commanders to fire at their discretion."

"Air Force?"

"They've got everything airborne to engage potential alien dropships. Same as the Navy and Marines. All field forces are deployed for combat."

She tried to think if there was anything else to throw at this invading entity.

"Ma'am," someone called out. "The President is on the line."

General Clark waved that off.

"Space Command is reporting all satellites the Core has passed are no longer functional," another subordinate reported. "GPS no longer works."

More trivia in the face of doom.

"Space Command said that the mothership that launched from Area 51 has, well, disappeared."

That drew her focus. "Destroyed?"

"No, ma'am. Just vanished."

Clark nodded. "Good. Turcotte got those people away. Good. Then there is still hope for mankind."

The Core was over the west coast.

EARTH ORBIT

The mothership had been there one moment, gone the next, as it shifted into FTLT.

Turcotte was momentarily shocked at the abrupt disappearance. Then experienced a brief relief that some sliver of humanity had escaped washed through him.

That sliver evaporated as multiple particle beams flashed past, firing at the spot where the mothership had just occupied. His muscles tightened as he expected his ship to be blasted when the Core shifted aim.

But nothing. The Core resumed firing downward toward the planet.

Turcotte relaxed his shoulders as much as he could. Perhaps the *Fynbar* was as 'invisible' to the Core as it had been to the Airlia systems?

Turcotte gasped as pain spiked through his brain, originating from the base of his skull to right between his eyes. For a moment he thought the craft had been hit and he'd been struck by shrapnel. He reached up and felt the back of his head, his forehead. No blood. No obvious wound. Nothing. But the pain remained, pulsing. A live wire vibrating through center of his brain.

The implant!

It was a quarter inch diameter ball in the back of his brain, just above the stem that had only recently discovered via MRI when he'd been prepared for fitting of his TASC-suit. There was also a microscopic line extending from it running to his cerebrum. But what it did? The doctors had not been able to tell him. And then Lisa Duncan, in her farewell note to him confessed that she believed she'd implanted it, although she had no conscious memory of the act.

Turcotte took a deep breath while he closed his eyes, waiting for some sort of image to develop, a message, anything.

But there was only throbbing pain.

What was the implant doing?

Why had it activated for the first time?

What was it supposed to do?

Turcotte opened his eyes and realized that during that brief period, the Battle Core had continued to approach and was barely one hundred miles away. It was rapidly coming toward him. He grabbed the controls and turned the *Fynbar* toward Earth.

This war was far from over.

AREA 51: INVASION

COPYRIGHT

Cool Gus Publishing

www.bobmayer.com

This is a work of fiction. Names, characters, places, and incidents either are the product of the author's imagination or are used fictitiously, and any resemblance to actual persons living or dead, business establishments, events, or locales is entirely coincidental.

EQUINOX by Bob Mayer
COPYRIGHT © 2020 by Bob Mayer

·ontent com/pod-product-compliance
ıce LLC
PA
70626
)07B/2702